I0829501

TOGETHER THE FUTURE
With Stories by Gabriela, Sabina and Nadia Hobbs

ISBN: 978-0-6484476-7-2

The authors would like to thank Michael Carroll, Fellow, IAAA, author and artist and David A. Hardy, FBIS (Hon) and Fellow, IAAA for their assistance with this book.

Dedicated to the Mars Society Australia, currently cared for by Jonathan and Anna Clarke.

(Preceding page) A fleet of probes prepare to comb the galaxy in search for life, receiving a gravity assisted boost from a nearby planet.
(Facing page) The ancient remains of a generational starship orbits silently above an inhabited world.

FOREWORD
By Michael Carroll

Time travel is a tricky thing. Einstein's math does not preclude it, but it has not, as yet, given us an easy way to do it. We can travel into the future by traveling at faster-than-light speeds. For us, time will slow, and for the place of our departure, it will continue. When we return, we will return to our future. Travel into the past, that's a bit more dicey. Will I change things? Enigmas like the Grandfather paradox (Can I go back and kill my grandfather, which leads to me not being around to kill him?) bother us logically, and travel into the past is beyond our current capabilities.

That's where archeology comes in. In a quite visceral sense, archeology helps us see back in time, puts us on the streets of ancient Santorini before Thera blew her top, or upon the sands of the Sinai in time to see Tutankamun's burial parade.

And thanks to modern technology, we have the Galactic Museum of History. Within its twelve stories, you'll visit the dark years of the Bio wars, the plucky artificial chicken Noosh, the mysterious ruins in the deserts of Mars, the exciting first discovery of intelligent life beyond Earth on a moon of Herculis, and the glorious meeting of two cultures on the Irs homeworld.

Through the eyes of the fine artist Steven Hobbs and the inspiring edits of Gabriela, Sabina and Nadia Hobbs, take a journey across the galaxy, through the ages, and into realms of fiction informed by science. Part Twilight Zone and part Star Wars, it is a wild and wonderful ride.

Michael Carroll
Fellow, International Association of Astronomical Artists, author and artist

Parker, Colorado, USA January 2022

CONTENTS

The Museum..6

The Forgotten Soldier...8

The Foxhound..16

The Red War..24

The Fall..30

The Pyramids of Mars...36

The Kane Warp Drive..44

The Unusual Suspect..50

The Wings of Legend..60

From Red to Green...70

The Exodus..76

The Rescuers...84

The New Start..92

A Peep Through the Fog.......................................94

The End of Night..100

What You Bring With You....................................104

Family Squabbles...110

The Final Battle.. 118

The Awakening...126

Hosting a Museum..134

THE MUSEUM

"Welcome to the Galactic Museum of History. Spanning across 12 floors you will find the culmination of decades of dedicated work of archaeologists travelling across galaxies. Whether it is an ancient artefact resting on the sands of a war-shattered planet or a new race existing outside of our known world, these novel pieces of historic puzzle are being found and placed together to form a magnificent story of our past.

Here you will also see the latest results of generations of historians who spent thousands of years solving age-old puzzles..."

Ethan dismissed the museum's virtual assistant with a flick of his hand.

"Can we do something else? I'm hungry," the pre-teen complained.

"Maybe you should think of more than your stomach," countered Sophie, Ethan's older sister. Unlike her brother, she took a keen interest in the museum's impressive exhibits.

They came across what looked like an old soldier's combat suit, complete with bulbous helmet and gas mask.

"What is the point of wearing this costume?" Ethan taunted. "You could hardly see out of that hideous helmet and that rusty rifle looks like it weighs a ton."

Amateur historian Sophie tried to explain. "Back during the Bio Wars, the Earth's atmosphere was poisonous, so you had to fight in a protected suit."

Another virtual assistant appeared. "The military had to fight the Bions who, part human, part something else, almost destroyed society as we know it."

A brightly coloured exhibit caught Ethan's eye. "The Bions couldn't have been that ferocious if they fought with robot chickens."

Sophie tried to ignore her brother and moved to a cabinet containing a battered electronic combat diary and a large medallion, still gleaming after all this time. She had just made out the work "Foxhound" in the inscription before her brother grabbed her hand and pulled her away.

"Come on, food, remember?"

"There you are!" Exton, the children's older brother, had just burst out of the Mars exhibit and rushed up to meet them.

"You should have seen it!" he exclaimed. "It was just like you were there. You had to wear the same type of old space suits the early explorers had, and you were surrounded with

wall-to-wall red dust and pink skies, just like the land was before the Martian terraforming."

"Did you do the ruins tour or go to the Pyramids?" asked Sophie disappointed not to have seen the landscape as she was looking after Ethen.

"The Pyramids," Exton replied, ignoring Ethan's bored look. "They were massive, five of them sitting there in the red dust It took forever before anyone could find out what was inside them was incredible."

"The alien remains discovery of the century, and a devastating asteroid strike didn't help matters," Sophie said to herself as much as to the group.

At this point Ethan had given up on his siblings and began to make a beeline straight for the Museum's cafeteria. Before he got too far, Sophie grabbed his hand and yanked him back.

"We have to wait until Mom and Dad are finished in the Exodus exhibit, remember?" Sophie said by way of explanation. She couldn't hide her disappointment of missing out on yet another exhibit, being forced to look after her younger brother. She had also shuffled the trio to an interim exhibit on the way to the larger Exodus displays.

Let's look at the first alien spaceship our ancestors discovered soon after the invention of the Kane Warp Drive," she offered, hoping to see something useful while waiting. The display was well structured even though only a fragment of the real spacecraft was present.

Three-dimensional projections filled in the blanks to make the trio believe they were looking at all of the vessel, partially submerged in an alien crater.

Exton moved for a closer look. He shared some of the history passion his sister had. "I think the original crew of this spaceship went mad."

"Yes," cut in Sophie. "That is how it got where it was…."

Before she could explain further, her parents appeared to step right on top of the virtual scene as they walked over to their children.

"Hi folks! Hungry?" Ethan's father said, sharing his younger son's interest in food. "Seeing life on board an Exodus ship built an appetite."

"Imagine spending your whole life doing your job, then after you die, someone else does exactly the same work, then someone new after that…for generations," Sophie's mother added thoughtfully.

"I don't know how they could stand it," added Sophie's older brother. "To know that almost none of what they did contributed anything to their survival."

Sophie's father stifled a yawn. "Sounds like my day job actually, but none of this is getting us fed. To the Cafeteria!"

With that he and Ethan strode purposely in the general direction of the Museum's food court, the rest of the family reluctantly following behind. Sophie's mother saw Sophie's disappointment in not being able to see the rest of the museum. She leaned closer to her daughter's face: "Once we all finish stuffing our faces, why don't you take Exton to the New Discoveries area? I heard a new post-Exodus civilisation exhibit is about to open, and Cameron Breen is personally opening it."

"What, the son of Captain Breen, Terran ambassador who made first personal intergalactic contact?" Exclaimed Sophie, her eyes wide.

"The same," her mother affirmed, realising her daughter would remember this for the rest of her life.

Much later, well after food, after the legendary meeting with Cameron Breen and after many lengthy visits to other exhibits, an exhausted Sophie started thinking how she really liked the museum, and dreamed of one day opening her own exhibition on some far away world. There seemed to be plenty of opportunities, with missions pushing further into deep space.

Slowly wandering back, Sophie found herself again in front of the ancient bio suit. She saw her reflection in the pitted helmet visor, wondering what the owner of this suit had experienced in the Bio Wars, particularly during the early period leading up to the conflict. She couldn't help but think how technology gone wrong, coupled with lack of resources and civil unrest that led to disastrous consequences.

THE FORGOTTEN SOLDIER

(Above) In the early phases of the war, confident soldiers enjoyed the protection of supporting airpower and mobile artillery. This assumed superiority dwindled over a period of months, as critical supplies were destroyed by the adversary and soldiers resorted to guerilla warfare.

The events leading up to what has been labeled as the most violent struggle in recorded times are best described through the lives of many people who lived during the Bio Wars. Such a man is Lieutenant Mark Anderson whose impressive electronic war diary has recorded multiple military and personal events. The following passages were taken from Lt. Anderson's diary, which portrayed the war on the ground through the perspective of an ordinary troop commander.

July 9

 I don't know what I'm doing here. A couple of months ago everything was just normal. Normal work, normal food, normal life. Then they announced the war, and suddenly my life changed. I found myself undergoing harsh military training. That dreaded enrolment took me and many others by surprise, though we should have seen it coming. Yet, none of us ever thought that a group of lunatics could seriously impact our world, our future.

For years, we had known of the experiments involving human-nerve-tissue integration with organic circuitry. We were also aware people were crazy enough to join their brain to a computer chip. Scientists tried to produce the 'perfect being' which pretended to be the next evolutionary step for humanity – a natural combination of best humans and most performant robotic elements. But at that time, we had no idea they were crazy enough to genetically modify the human body in accordance with their mixed-race ideology and that a secret army was actively supporting it. By then, they had been building up their military robotic forces for years. It wasn't until the first town was obliterated and thousands of innocent people were murdered, that we finally got their annihilation message. Our 'normal' is now over and I'm sure many dangerous days are about to come.

As I sit with fifty other people, some teenagers, in our small crib room full of sweating bodies, I am ready to fight our common enemy since such fighting is personal, for our individual freedom, and ultimately for own survival. Scattered among us are weapons of all sorts, ration packs and few personal belongings. Overhead, a single battery is powering a fluorescent hanging tube illuminating this tiny room. Everyone is tired, including me, as we have endured a hard day of orientation and training. Fear and nervousness lurk behind our eyes, for tomorrow we are to face our first combat mission as a newly formed operational unit. I am so nervous since I am their leader and responsible for their lives. I know I'm not worthy of their command, but still very proud to be of use, even if only to keep up the morale. Surely there are better, more qualified soldiers than me to lead the fight.

July 12

Since my last entry, my unit has undergone numerous missions. At 0400 hours, on the 10th, my unit broke base and, using an all-terrain tactical vehicle as transport, entered a 'hot zone' nearby. I remember looking at all my soldiers and sensing the absolute terror within their minds. I wondered if Bions felt this kind of anguish before each battle?

Command has deemed the area we were sent into as a low-risk and thought in all their wisdom that it would be safe for us to be inducted into combat. From that point I quickly learnt that nowhere is safe. For unknown reasons, the enemy has increased their activity here, well above what Command had predicted.

During the first few minutes, six of my command were already wounded by the Bions. I saw my enemy for the first time. They were horrid things; their bodies were unnatural and seemed liked monsters. Yet, here they were, not far from our transport and causing havoc.

After I rushed my team to cover, I watched a Bion in combat. It was tough and seemed more skilled than my entire unit put together. Luckily, after a few seconds of constant firing, this Bion went down. It was clear that our current arms – 'toys' as my second in command called them, were outdated compared to their weapons. A great improvement will be needed if we want to have a chance at defeating them.

After depleting nearly half our ammunition, we finally secured our position and called Command for a Position Compromise Extraction (PCE). However, the increased threat in the area was enough for Headquarters to deny our request and force us to move to the nearest safe radio spot some kilometres away. Every minute in that place caused me to lose more of my sanity. I had to leave some of my wounded behind. Incoming Bion re-enforcements threatened to wipe out my entire unit. It was hard to believe that not long ago the place had been filled with people happily going about their business. Instead, we cringed within the derelict buildings in fear of death. The only movement my unit could do was to cautiously make its way forward.

After the first two days I have noticed that we are starting to work as a team. There is nothing like a combat situation to bring out someone's true nature and the absolute dependence on each other. Simple things such as reliving oneself with four guards surrounding you helped the bonding process of my small unit. It was on the third day when we ran into real trouble. We were only two kilometres from our pick-up point when Teddy, our Airborne Threat Lookout guy (whom we called ATL) screamed:

"Inbound!"

Without thinking, we all quickly dived for cover and looked up to see two Sky-Sharks screaming through the air. Their engines were deafening us as they flew above us. Their ultra-fine sensors picked up our body temperature from long range and stealthily approached us until they were on-top of us. We were petrified that the Bions would lock onto our body positions and shoot us where we crouched. Our ground-to-air defender, Sally-Anne, was quick though. She locked onto the first Sky-Shark and put a missile in the air before they had a chance to beam us. Her action was pure reflex and she didn't even remember placing the missile in the launcher, nor firing it.

The rest of us weren't far behind when the sky was lined with missiles and bullets released from down below. Our commando, Johnno, radioed for help.

Then, time slowed down as the Sky-Sharks gracefully soared through our metal rain and fired two air-to-ground rockets at us. Fortunately, their targeting was off, but by then, they were close enough to use their close-in guns.

As per training, I ordered my unit to spread out in order to make it harder for them to pick us off. Teddy was a bit too slow. He had been trading his position for another when he became the primary target for the second Sky-Shark. We gave him plenty of support fire, but it still wasn't enough as the enemy craft spun around and tracked him. I yelled a warning to poor Teddy, but it was too late. He got caught by their bullets in mid-air. Teddy's body was shredded to pieces. I can still see the look on his face as he saw the target beam locked onto his chest. In the last instant between life and death, when he was totally paralysed, his eyes were the only ones moving in a desperate call for help, a help that none of us could give. Then he was gone, disintegrating in a red shower of flesh and blood. I remember my body shaking while focusing my strength on the annihilation of the Sky-Sharks.

If it weren't for the hidden missile launchers Johnno had called in, who knows what would have happened to my unit. I cheered as one after the other, the Sky-Sharks went down in flames. My relief was brief as I looked over to where Teddy's remains were. The others followed my gaze and my unit fell silent as we all realised that although we had won the battle, it was at a dear cost. I had just lost another life under my command and many more might follow poor Teddy.

After completing the grizzly task of gathering Teddy's identification tag, we were again forced to move. I and my entire unit spent the entire trip pondering over the Sky-Shark battle and our own morality. I'm not sure if I ever will properly recover from my first experience in hell.

July 23

In the past ten days, my unit has completed three more missions, during which we have spent the time fighting non-stop. Then we somehow found ourselves in a rest-period between missions. Some of my men preferred to simply lay down, while others, such as Sally-Anne, are playing games now and laughing like there isn't a war on. Their enjoyment is pleasing to see and soothing, as it proves that humour is still present in this inferno. Although I long to join them, I am still trying to plan our next tactical mission movement as orders come in. Somehow, the stiffness of military bearing doesn't weigh down on me in the battlefield where everyone, no matter their rank seems on equal ground. For now, I must be content with simply watching their relaxation mood.

September 9

This diary is the only way I can keep track of time; all the days seem to merge into one seemingly endless combat. When you walk out of your base, you wonder whether this will be your last day and the terror of war makes it impossible to distinguish day from night. My unit is new to the Bio War.

The more missions we undertake, I am convinced that we are not doing well. There seem to be three more Bions to replace every one we destroy. We are slowly being pushed backwards by an enemy that shows no mercy. Our best tactics, firepower and maneuvers don't quite match our enemy. They are slowly destroying everything in their path in order to achieve their goal, whatever that might be.

During these past two months, my unit has shifted base three times after our previous locations were discovered and destroyed by the enemy. My unit has found that the key to survival is to keep moving. I am pretty used to this now.

Yesterday, my last maneuver was a very sudden one. A surprise attack left five squads scurrying for cover with many members slaughtered, while the rest of us hurried through to another zone. Two squads made it; the rest were picked off one by one. My unit lost two great men: Sam and Freddie. Sam was hit by a remote sniper while we were on a food stop. One second, he was eating with us and the next his lifeless torso fell to the ground. He had just turned 21 and was talking about his birthday celebration the day before. Now I have to plan his funeral when or if we return home.

Freddie at least had a chance to fight back. On the second leg of our journey, my unit ran into an ambush of four Bions who pinned us on all sides. Freddie broke under pressure and leaped up and out, screaming obscenities at the top of his lungs. He was deaf to our cries and numb to the hits he took. He fired madly at the nearest Bion until his weapon jammed. I think he would have thrown rocks at the Bions if he still had his arms by then. Perhaps the most amazing thing was that Freddie had been the quietest of us. Maybe this is why none of us thought him capable of such bravery.

At the debriefing afterwards, Freddie was commended for his honourable act, but I saw no glory in it. I only saw a 16-year-old hacked to pieces by an unfeeling monster who didn't care who it shot at.

October 8

The past month of fighting has steadily gotten worse; I continue to lose ground and men to the enemy. I am fighting with only 60% of soldiers I had a few months ago. I think each one of us suspects that they might die on the battlefield - it's only a matter of time and how.

The average life span of a solider in this war seems to be a few weeks, though a sergeant managed to survive a record of six months and five days. I am hoping to beat this record and so is my unit, whose ultimate goal is survival. This allows us all to aim for something and not flee. It also boosts our morale.

A combination of both pollution and enemy attacks has made this battlefield an increasingly hostile environment. As a result, we have all been issued environmental suits, although I think an anti-beaming overall might be a better fit. It is now a rare day to go without full protective gear. Nevertheless, I've seen what those chemicals can do to a person: it rots you from inside out when you inhale those toxins. The damage is worse when the chemicals touch the skin. The pain is overwhelming to watch or listen to; nobody wants to die in agony.

November 4

I have lost more soldiers since my last diary entry; they were new recruits and I can't even remember their names. They still haven't been replaced and my unit is always fighting short. This means we're starting to double up on duties and my command is being affected by this measure. My orders are coming less regularly, and more responsibility is being placed on me to come up with my own tactics. How can we possibly win this war if our leaders no longer know what they are doing, and our units are slowly falling apart?

We were deploying to an abandoned house when Sally-Anne came across a badly damaged child's doll, laying amongst other debris. She picked it up and turned to me with a strange expression. She muttered to me about how it belonged to someone's child, someone who never grew up. Then the next instant she collapsed onto the ground rocking back and forth, bursting into tears. After a while, I sat down with her and cradled her in my arms while she slept. I think I also might have cried too. We undoubtedly must have looked strange to my unit. Two highly skilled soldiers weeping over a scruffy doll that belonged to a child we never knew.

November 23
We had a surprise attack on my base yesterday and less than half of us got out. We made a fighting retreat while running for a safer zone. It seems as though the Bions will not rest until all military units are discovered and killed.

As we were running, I happened to glance in Sally-Anne's direction. As I saw her sprinting for her life, like the rest of us, an overwhelming sense of protectiveness surged through my veins. It was something over and above the usual duty of care I had towards my unit. I then realised how much I would miss her if I lost her. There is a special bond between us which has been strengthened by the fact that we are now the only two original people left in my unit. Now I think I'm becoming attracted to her. I realise that this is ridiculous as neither of us has a chance of living long enough to develop a proper relationship. Furthermore, I am her lieutenant and I must be her leader and not her lover.

December 25
It's Christmas Day and those who aren't on guard are celebrating. Although there isn't much to be happy about, my soldiers are managing somehow. Even I have loosened myself enough to fool around with the guys and girls, playing out season compliments for all they were worth. Modified helmets have become party hats and various trinkets from rubbish piles have been wrapped and traded as gifts. Even in the darkest of hours, humanity can find a way to light up.

As I watch everyone singing carols and enjoying themselves, I think about the enemy. Would they observe or even remember the season that had played such an important role in human history? Or would it just be another time for them to fight and bring their forces one step closer to the victory they are so close to achieving?

As I put in these words, I look at Sally-Anne flirting with other men from my unit. She catches my eye and then quickly looks away. I'm sure she suspects something. I'm so close to telling her how I feel - we have nothing to lose anyway. Yet, I can't help wondering if it will affect my performance as a leader and endanger lives, including hers.

December 26
Our celebrations are over, and fighting has begun once more. On Christmas night numerous bases were hit and many people died. It seems as though the Bions have lost all the humanity they had left. They no longer feel compassion, but they have lost none of their cunning or strength. We must always be prepared for the worst and fight back at any time. Anyway, for my unit, the Christmas miracle happened as we were never caught off guard since Christmas's Eve.

January 1
The first day of a new year. What will this dreadful year hold for us? Who will be the victor this time? I doubt this war can go on for any longer; we are down to less than a third of our original force. This has become further spread out as we resort to different tactics against the Bions. They have reduced our losses significantly but have also made us less effective in our strikes. The human race is in serious

(Above) The relentless pressure and deteriorating strategic situation had a heavy impact on the remaining soldiers.

trouble and the only way to prevent that is to fight an impossibly strong and vicious enemy.

Tonight, we have decided to take advantage of a lull in enemy attacks and have a small party to celebrate the New Year's. We all need a boost in morale and some relaxation now more than ever.

January 2

I finally did it! I told Sally-Anne how I felt. During our New Year's party, I took a small detachment consisting of Sally-Anne and myself to patrol the surrounding area. I made sure that our patrol took us to a small building I found earlier and soon we were inside. We took off our protective gear for a brief rest when I finally found the courage to have a personal talk with her. The rest of that time glowed like a small light in the darkness.

When we returned from our patrol, we behaved as normal since it's better for both of us to put feelings aside if we are to survive. No one knows about our relationship although I think my unit suspects something, but like good mates, they pretended not to know, which made it easier for us both.

March 2

I have lost my Sally-Anne. I feel empty as a part of me dies with her out there. Perhaps writing about how it occurred might help me come to grips with my loss and overcome pain. Five days ago, we were out on one of our most ambitious missions yet. The plan was to ambush and capture a heavily armed ground vehicle used by our enemy. With one of these we could destroy the Bions using their own technology. Then, with tactical upper hand, we might have a chance of victory against these monsters.

There were three units involved, sixteen soldiers in all. We had managed to 'borrow' some high explosives from an enemy stockpile on a previous mission. We planned to use it to immobilise the target. Then we would attempt to break into the crippling machine and try to hijack the beaming technology. The theory side of the plan was good, and it would have worked perfectly, if it weren't for the Sky-Sharks that escorted the target vehicle.

They must have seen us while we were setting up our traps and let us finish before they came screaming in. The sound of their engines could send any grown person insane. When you hear that buzzing metallic sound you know that someone will vanish, possibly even yourself.

I saw several men virtually disappear in a second, wiped out where they crouched. That was when I remembered Teddy. Teddy was killed by those Sky-Sharks.

Those of us who weren't immediately killed put up a hell of a fight. Sally-Anne had her faithful missile launcher on her shoulder and as we ran, she fired madly behind her to give us time to hide for cover. One of the attackers was disabled and I almost reached her when the second Sky-Shark found its target: Sally-Anne.

She was blown twenty metres into the air and then landed with a sickening thud. Time seemed to stop and my senses went numb. The Sky-Shark must have thought that the impact had outright killed her because it banked away, looking for other victims. By the time it was out of range, I was at Sally-Anne's side. She had been hit by shrapnel from the blast and her body was in a torn mess from the waist down. When her dulling eyes registered my presence, she tried to speak but only blood came out. She looked at me with pleading eyes and I understood. Sally-Anne closed her eyes and tears fell.

March 12

Yesterday the five of us that survived the Sky-Shark attack met up with another unit, and now we at least have a temporary base. There are now only twelve people when there used to be fifty. Orders from my Command are gone now, so we are more or less commanding ourselves. Soon there will be no Command and no one left to fight for humanity. Then, the Bions will win.

While on a brief stop, I've moved away from the others and am thinking about all this. The pain, the suffering and the screams. I too scream at night. The screams that everyone makes when a Sky-Shark appears. I have come to the end of my endurance.

I pointed my weapon to my head and began to squeeze the trigger. Just before the hammer fired the round, I instinctively jerked away. The bullet missed me by millimetres. It was then when I realised that I still wanted to live. I still want to feel the wind brushing my skin.

April 4

We now are trying to catch a few hours of sleep between missions. After an hour of trying, I have given up. Every time I close my eyes, I see Sally-Anne and have nightmares. So instead, I've gone outside to gaze at the war-stricken streets that were once bursting with activity.

As I look out at the smoky sky, I think of Sally-Anne, Sam, Teddy and so many other friends.

I also know that each sunset brings me closer to them.

Lt Anderson was assessed to have perished two weeks after his last diary entry. He also came in close contact with the Foxhound, the person responsible for ending the Bio War.

(Above) Two soldiers, caught in the open, desperately return fire at the airborne threat with twin-barrelled Boltzmann rifles. These semi-guided weapons proved surprisingly effective against Bions.

THE FOXHOUND

(Above) Towards the end of the Bio war, it was the Bions' turn to suffer shortages of war materiel. A wheeled rover inspects a service robot destroyed by the Foxhound's team.

Six pairs of feet made their way heavily across uneven ground. Five suited figures followed their leader through the battlefield as a silver-grey streak pierced the air.

"Inbound!" the dust rose as a single word penetrated each soldier's ears. Without even thinking, I motioned for the men to continue to flee. In this war there was only time for quick decisions on how to save those close to you.

I unslung my weapon with trembling mind, yet very firm hands as I aimed it carefully at a rapidly approaching aircraft. My shoulders jerked involuntarily as I let off several rounds. Then, without bothering to see if I hit anything, I turned and ran in the direction of the others.

"Launch! Launch!"

Someone's voice reached my bleeding ears as they franticly signaled that the aircraft had released a missile at us. My heart pounded as I turned and saw death streaking towards me, leaving a ghostly white trail behind it. Everyone had found cover except me - I was the only one in the open.

My face met the ground just as the world around me erupted in a blinding flash.

The air smells sweet and my fingertips feel the soft grass. Everything seems perfect. My wife and my best friend are with me. Then the clear sky turns bleak.

A Bion makes its way towards us.

"Michael! Do something!"

My best friend stood up in a shooter's stance, his missile launcher to his shoulder. I tried to follow his lead, but my legs gave way and I fell back down. Multiple shots ripped through his body, but he still kept fighting for me.

Then he fell…like when he did 47 years ago, when the Bions attacked Sector 14.

Michael's eyes shot open and slowly adjusted to the bright sunlight streaming through the window. He wiped his sweaty palms as it dawned to him that the nightmare had passed, and that he was safe once more.

It was always the same dream that woke him, always popping up. With clockwork regularity, the nightmare interrupted his sedentary life and graphically reminded him of how close he had come to death that awful day. Fortunately, his last dive had sent him over a large outcrop that absorbed most of the blast.

His thoughts were abruptly broken by the sound of footsteps that rapidly approached. His wife, Jackie, warily peeped her head around the corner:

"Michael, Michael! Are you okay? I thought I heard you shouting." Her worried voice tinkled against the walls. She was once the most beautiful woman on earth and to Michael, she was still as charming as the day he had chased her down that bombed-down street many years before.

"I'm fine," Michael's hoarse voice sounded unconvincing. "It was only that dream again."
The fact was that Michael had been suffering from this particular nightmare for decades. Even so, Jackie always came running to his side when he woke with a yell. Michael thought it was some sort of crazy passion and he loved her for it. After stroking her husband's hair, Jackie started to relax and lapse back into one of her infamous teasing moods.

"Well, if that's all, come and get ready, lazy head. Skye is coming again with her kids for mid-rations." Jackie smiled weakly as Michael sighed heavily and made a show of how hard it was to get up.

"Lunch, Jackie, lunch. Not even your cooking is as bad as the old mid-rations." Michael ducked as a pillow came whistling for his head. He proceeded to get ready while wondering what story he was going to tell his grandchildren that day. A pang hit his heart as he remembered that the two boys had lost their father from radiation-induced complications, and also the great pain their mother experienced following his son's death.

Michael liked to tell his war stories with humor, and took a certain amount of pride in keeping the boys captivated by his narratives. They were always straight-faced and attentive whilst listening to him, though that might have been due to Skye's influence. Yet, when Michael looked into their eyes, he could detect a look of amazement. What had been a real and terrifying experience for himself and his wife, was now an adventure story to his grandsons. In a way he was glad for this, thinking the less they appreciated the torment and pain involved, the better.

Suddenly, two pairs of eager footsteps ran through the hall into the study where their grandfather spent most of his time. The walls were decorated with various memorabilia and in the centre, on the mantelpiece, stood Michael's most prized weapon: the twin-barrelled Boltzmann assault rifle.

As the young boys, Sam and Jake, eagerly propped themselves on twin couches, their eyes remained glued upon the gun. Despite how much they wished to handle it, the grandfather never permitted it: "Only when you are adults will I let you hold it, as it is dangerous and a weapon you should hope never to fire." Michael's words of caution were said whenever they paid too much attention to the Boltzmann.

Michael smiled weakly as he entered his study with his daughter, the boys' mother, Skye. Like her mother, Skye's face was also worn from stress despite being younger. The generation following the Bio Wars was contending with reconstruction, as well as radiation effects.

Skye raised her children alone through all of this. Michael and Jackie helped where they could. "Grandad, Grandad; tell us more war stories! Who were your enemies? Where did they come from? Why did you have to fight them?" their enthusiastic voices chorused as one.

Laughing softly to himself, Michael began to tell his story as one of adventure and excitement, quite the opposite of struggle for survival, trauma and loss: "Do you remember when I told you about the group of crazy scientists? They wanted to be better than everyone else, live longer and thought they could be smarter too. They threw away their bodies and some of them disposed of their brains too."

Exciting storytelling and painful memories merged. The 'crazy' scientists were in fact legitimate researchers. Their funded program meant wholesale replacement of body parts by sophisticated robotic parts or 'bionic prosthetics'.

"They wanted to live forever and never get hurt. There would also be no need to drink, eat or sleep since they would never get tired, nor hungry," Michael said, feigning excitement.

"Soon almost everyone wanted in on this new fad. The disabled people, the athletes and even everyday people wanted to hack off their own limbs and replace them with robotic parts to better themselves."

Michael shook the memory away as the two boys winced at the thought of cutting one's own limb off for fun. They involuntarily drew their arms and legs closer to themselves - an action that didn't surprise Michael.

"I'm serious, they thought it was a good thing!" Michael cringed as he continued with his story.

"Soon, the crazy scientists involved in these experiments decided that they were better than everyone else because they were in fact stronger, healthier and could even live longer! The rest of us thought we were in fact the superior ones because they were more human, more prone to danger."

Michael remembered that in almost no time, two distinct groups of people had emerged and philosophical arguments raged as to whether humanity was now two separate species. Government policy and even leadership across the world struggled to work through what had just happened. More dangerous positions started to emerge – like the one on which 'species' should be dominant and likewise which should be the one governed by the first group.

Silly proposals arose on classifying people by amount of original body type versus robotic parts, but soon the development of purpose-built fighters, 'bions', abruptly ended the philosophical debates. With no warning, the mostly-robots attacked the mostly-humans. Then, an elite squad broke into a key facility and used the bions to break the attack. The Bions happily obliged, and then kept going.

"The mostly-humans and mostly-robots got a nasty surprise when their 'loyal servants' decided not to care who or what they attacked," Michael almost smiled retelling this surprise and extremely nasty turn of events. Had the bions listened to the commands, history wouldn't have recorded this 'engineering' retribution so tragically.

"We fought long and hard, but we had to eat and sleep, while the Bions didn't," said Michael.

"But the Foxhound save us, right?" interrupted Sam. His face was covered in concern as to whether the Bions had truly won.

"Of course, he did, and I was with him when he saved us," Michael grinned. Jackie let out a giggle from the doorway; it was quite rare seeing Michael looking so proud.

Michael once again began his tale, but more softly than before, "The fighting had gotten really bad for us. All we could do was sneak attacks onto our enemies. We would run out, do as much damage as we could and then return to our hiding places.

"One day, six of us led by the Foxhound tried to make a surprise attack on a couple of tanks. But our attempt went downhill fast. We were forced to retreat, with the enemy hard on us. For days we were forced to run until we reached the surrounding hills. There, we stayed hidden until the enemy left. But, instead of going back down to fight, the Foxhound kept leading us further to the hills without telling us the reason!"

"We did not know at the time, but he was leading us to his secret hideout. Far from the battlefield and even further from home. The Foxhound stopped us at a ridge and told us to dig. Nothing else, no explanation; only the words dig as he stared at the map in his hands."

As Michael recounted his experience, his mind wandering in the past as if he was once more on that ridge, digging into the rocky soil.

His kit spade had hit an obstruction and he quickly alerted the men. The Foxhound looked forward with his eyes blazing and the men took this as a sign that they had nearly reached their goal. Soil was rapidly cleared to reveal a rusty metal hatch. Despite all the soldiers' strength combined, they could not force open the hatch, so the Foxhound ordered it to be blown open. Michael and the rest took cover.

The smoke had barely cleared when the Foxhound leaped forward. Peering into the space beyond the hatch, Michael noticed a tunnel with a metal ladder leading down into darkness. Cautiously, the Foxhound led them down into the gloom. Lights were switched on, revealing rows and rows of electronic equipment sealed in plastic bags to prevent corrosion. Although they looked as primitive as abacuses, Michael later understood that they held the key to victory. He noticed that he was panting slightly, the oxygen levels inside the facility had been deliberately kept low to prevent further erosion. The men were led into a circular room dominated by a huge missile.

Michael's gaze unwillingly followed the missile's sleek contours upwards until they were lost above him. Yet, there was no time to marvel as the Foxhound quickly barked orders.

All the equipment lying untouched for decades was quickly unwrapped. It was only after the old systems were operational that the Foxhound told them about his plan. Fragments of that age-old conversation flashed through Michael's head: "10 megaton nuclear guided missile…one of the dozens scattered through the world…automatically networked and linked to this one…other silos already being prepped as we speak…hit the Bions so hard they won't recover".

One by one, the consequences of the Foxhound's plan dawned on the team. Could this stop the Bions?

"We worked in that old silo, deep underground," said Michael.

"How did you know where the silo was?" Sam asked.

Michael remembered the reason, simple enough as it happened. "The Foxhound's father used to be a member of a special war party that had loathed the disarmament policies brought in by the officials at the time. Instead of disarming the nuclear missiles like they were meant to, the Foxhound's father and some of his friends stole some and hid them in various places for 'protection'. Their locations were only known by their small secret network, and it was by accident that the Foxhound had learnt about their location after his father died."

(Left) A 'missing man' formation is flown over one of the many memorials that appeared after the conclusion of the war.

Michael looked away from his grandsons, he felt bitter for lying to them. In truth, the Foxhound had known about the nuclear silos eighteen years before the passing of his father. But Michael did not want to tarnish the Foxhound's heroic proportions. He didn't want his descendants to know how much of a coward the Foxhound actually was.

Despite his feelings, Michael continued his tale once more:

"Many months had passed since the discovery of the silo. The Foxhound's team had made their way home, venturing out only to steal supplies and communicate with other groups. Then, after waiting almost forever, a messenger returned with the long-awaited news; all the other silos were ready."

Returning to the silo, the Foxhound armed the link-up. Nearly all the missiles were targeting Tumboes - factories used by Bions to turn out new parts and machines to bolster their already swollen ranks. Michael remembered the newly manufactured Bions as no longer even being partly human, but merely sophisticated automatons, solely designed to kill people.

Launch keys were turned and an ancient missile, along with dozens of others, was sent on its way. Skimming the ground, the missile screamed towards its target at four times the speed of sound- a speed that rendered it untraceable to Bion weapons. The imposing bulk of its target loomed ahead and grew as the missile ate up the distance towards it.

The missile, the Tumbo and the surrounding area soon disappeared in a blinding fireball. Elsewhere, the scene was the same. Bion constructions that had been previously invulnerable to human attacks, fell before a mysterious and unstoppable avenger.

"We watched that fireball from on top of the silo, Michael said as his eyes lit up with an evil glint. "We watched our second sun eat up the enemy like it wasn't there."

Jackie, sensing the uneasiness in Michael and the grandchildren at this part of the 'story', curtly reminded them all that it was lunchtime.

Michael screwed up his face, "We'd better go or your grandmother will eat us alive!" As they all marched down to the dining area, Michael felt a tug on his shirt. He looked down at Sam.

"Grandad, what happened to the Foxhound, you know, after the war?"

Michael patted the youngster on the head, "I'm afraid he died soon after the missiles were launched. Even heroes cannot live forever".

"Well at least he stopped the war, didn't he Grandad?" the young child smiled.

"Yes, yes, he did," Michael dropped his gaze to the floor.

Of course, the war had not stopped right after the missiles were released. It took more hard years after their first true victory until humanity won back their world. However, the Bions' reproduction capabilities had been severely hampered by the human resistance's nuclear strikes and the humans finally had the advantage.

Michael had personally seen the last Bion fall - a crazed and dying machine attempting to repel the advancing human crowds. The people had moved as one and ripped the Bion apart with bare hands, hands that had experienced many years of torture and pain because of the unfeeling machines. The crowds continued to beat and smash the machine even after it had long ceased to twitch. Then what twisted material remained of the fallen Bion was thrown into the air and a rising scream of victory issued from hundreds of throats indicated that they were finally safe.

Michael suddenly woke up with a yell that startled Jackie who was sleeping soundly beside him. Even though the Bio War had finished decades ago, the memories still haunted him during the night. As Jackie stroked his arm, Michael smiled gently and felt grateful to have such an amazing woman by his side and returned his memory to better times like when they had first met: Michael and his team had been posted to Sector 14 almost 50 years ago. It had been one of the 500 war zones dividing the capital city during the war. When they first arrived, the sounds of multiple explosions choroused with the screams of dying people. Bright bursts of colours illuminated the sky, reminding Michael of the missiles sent by the Foxhound a few months before arriving to Sector 14.

His squad had been positioned there for reconnaissance purposes; they had just begun their mission when five raider ATVs suddenly came upon them. It was a disaster. Their whole unit might have ended up dead if it was not for another unit that had stumbled across their battle. One member of that unit was a fiery little woman by the name of Jackie. She had saved Michael from being killed numerous times afterwards.

Now, 47 years later, she looked at Michael with the same peculiar expression. "I've heard you telling the boys about the Foxhound," Jackie said cautiously.

"I told them that he was a great hero for what he did," Michael shifted nervously, "and that he died during the war".

"You lied to them? Why?"

"Because as far as I'm concerned the Foxhound is dead! I have and want no part of him anymore," Michael growled softly. He immediately felt guilty for snapping at Jackie when she retaliated:

"It's because of him that we are still here. Without him, our street would be a smoking ruin and we would probably be charred corpses!" Jackie stared out the window onto their street, built on top of Sector 14.

Michael sat up, "He knew of the existence of those nuclear silos for 20 years, Jackie. 20 years! Had he acted sooner; millions of people could still be alive".

Jackie glared at Michael, "It's not really his fault; he was weak, just human like the rest of us. Remember we were all fairly unrealistic about the threat".

Michael's burden seemed to lift slightly but he still fought, "That won't sound very convincing to the families of the dead. I am glad that I managed to suppress most of it after the war. It still wouldn't pay for everyone to know that the brave and heroic Foxhound had watched as the number of human corpses grew. I'm only glad that you stayed with me even after I told you the truth," Michael's sad eyes stared towards their old battle ground.

"You completed your mission and that's all that matters. Anyway, I think it is time to look forward, don't you?"

Later that night, Michael slipped silently out of bed, careful not to wake up his queen, and went to an adjacent room. He turned on a desk light and rummaged through Jackie's purse for a while and smiled sadly as he withdrew what he was looking for. A small black case. He knew that Jackie had brought it with her; she had done so since the end of the war when Michael had flatly refused to have anything to do with it. Now he ran his hands across its compact dimensions with a strange confidence he had never felt before. Finally, he sprung open the case's small lock and opened it to reveal a golden medallion, whose light he had not seen for 47 years.

He turned the medal within his old hands and forced himself to read the engravings at the back of it. They were simple words, but he had to fight an inner battle within himself before he could accept them: "To honour exceptional services above and beyond the call of duty, this token of gratitude is awarded to Michael L. Davis, the Foxhound."

THE RED WAR

(Above) Guided bombs are launched by the 'Breath-takers' towards targets near Valles Marineris, Mars. Fortunately, the scarce resources available to the on-orbit protagonists constrained the actual devastation caused in this small-scale conflict.

While the Bio Wars raged on Earth, a smaller scale conflict started on Mars. The inhabited colonies, suddenly cut off from their home-world, started developing automated warriors, or 'Breath-takers', to defend themselves. Before long the Breath-takers proved even more useful at removing rival colonists competing for scarce Martian resources. The Breath-takers were very efficient. Artificial intelligence, extreme mobility enhancements and virtually inexhaustible power sources often meant destroyed habitats were the only evidence of their existence. The rapidity of their actions made them almost impossible even for the remaining human colonists to observe them directly, let alone mount a good defence.

Not a day or even an hour passes without another murderous onslaught inside the impeccable white building called simply 'The Lab'. We are on the notorious Martian Short-Circuit Glacier, which is more of an island surrounded by ice. The origin of this island's name, however, remains obscure as there are few people left here to remember it. I and the few warriors near me live underground, free for the moment from the direct attacks of the Breath-takers. The Breath-takers haven't had it all their own way though. As they began to run out of human targets to destroy, they started to hunt each other. Some of the scientists here think it was some flaw in their artificial intelligence. Whatever the cause, their coordinated attacks on what remained of us broke down. Now their ruthless, mechanized discipline devolved into individual, mindless attacks on anything or nothing in particular.

We took our chance to bury ourselves below the surface and wait. We wanted the Breath-takers to kill enough of their own number so we could counter-attack. At least, that was how the warriors talked – has been for months. For me, this is my new home. I rarely go outside, for obvious reasons, and I am slowly forgetting what outside looks like. The warriors too have been getting restless, with air-launched bombing raids from the Breath-takers not helping anyone's patience.

This place, next to the glacier, is so cold, but for now, this doesn't seem to worry me, nor anyone else trapped inside this blockhouse. We are all more scared of the Breath-taker bombs dropping on us than some old myths of a serial killer let loose when people first colonised this island. The warriors started throwing around these stories as part of a joke to ease tensions. However, out of habit, I, too, lock my dormitory doors as the Martian sun sets and am very cautious not to venture far - even for a late snack or some conversation. This is kind of anti-social, at least for me, the technical assistant for professor Vadim. To make up for it I've got Noosh, a small robotic rooster which I had kind of adopted during my first night here. I don't really know where he (it?) came from; maybe this was some kind of spare-parts practical joke, or a half-finished artificial biology experiment. Either way this cockerel gives me a sense of security as he reminds me of my home town of Zavyalovo, in Siberia. So, after several months in this place, I've now got used to this spooky terrestrial habit of pretending to live with ghosts when there are none. Professor Vadim has not helped matters; his abrasive personality was made worse by being forced to abandon his work and laboratory at a moment's notice. I thought the alternative, rapid death by something that moved almost too fast to be seen, would have been worse but I dared not tell him that. So, I keep my silence, avoiding make-believe serial killers and trying not to pay attention to the war stories of the warriors who can't wait to fight. I am not even caring much about the other myths, simply because the mystery of a lonely killer gives birth to all sorts of weird talk, which I don't need if I am to enjoy my life here. This particular story centered on the Breath-takers. The warriors hated them all, and mostly with good reason. Not all artificial creations were killers though. Noosh is one of them, and our underground shelter has other mobile machines which we need to stay alive. The local legend says that this killer enjoyed dismantling helpful nuclear-powered robots for the sick pleasure of seeing the life fade out of their circuits…

"Progress done with stabilising the fourth nuclear reactor, Professor," I said with great joy after two-weeks of hard work. These reactors were very hard work – they were old, almost obsolete, but they were all we had to stay alive. Keeping just one reactor from either shutting down permanently or turning our base into a radioactive hole was almost a full-time job. Four temperamental reactors, on the other hand, were almost too much. So after nearly becoming radioactive myself after all this hard work, the professor simply gave me a nod and continued to work diligently on some green wires melted by solar microchips.

"Do you want me to check on our team?" I asked hoping to get an answer, as I knew the bombing attacks usually increased at lunch time.

"Oh, yes, yes, for sure!" came the half-distracted reply from my not so considerate leader. The team, or what was left of it, helped keep the facility operating while also doing scientific research between maintenance periods. Somehow, I thought the research was superfluous, and suspected it was done as more of a distraction. The team probably would not appreciate my suggestion of maintaining one of the four reactors as a distraction. Maybe then, I wouldn't be the only one to glow in the dark from radiation poisoning.

The bombing attack intensified, shaking our diamond-shaped habitat immensely. Each above-ground burst also destabilised the glacier, bit by bit. I wonder how long we had before being buried under a mountain of slushy ice. Despite the thoughts, I sounded cool and professional while I continued to greet my friends in a desperate effort to stay calm and in control of my increasing fear. Having my robot pet Noosh following me everywhere made this task much easier. My little companion cheered the team when he gave out 'mee-do-doos' that instead of 'cock-a-doodle-dos' and waited for a pat on his soft red crest, made out of synthetic rubber.

Then, Noosh stopped his robot rooster-call impersonations and started talking, saying something out of his character: "Why bomb this good-for-nothing place?"

"Oh," I wondered, "why indeed?"

So, why all this trouble? Why was it so vital for the enemy to put an end to our work? I asked myself. Was the research done in this little underground hideaway near a Martian glacier that important? If they waited long enough, the four temperamental reactors would probably finish us off anyway.

Then I realised the attackers were not after our technology. Even the capitulation and removal of our human team, held no interest to them. They were in fact after something much more precious than us and our lab: 'ice-blood' as it was called. Recently discovered by our team, buried deep inside this glacier, and as red as its human namesake, its origins are a mystery. Imagine a substance that can power better robots. It could revitalise an entire army of Breath-takers with even a tiny amount. Ice-blood was a very complex blend of nanotechnology and other compounds that could make killing machines even more powerful than the current generation of Breath-takers.

The ice-blood was many things: a temperature moderator, a powerful electric conductor, technology enhancer and damage repairer. Resistance against Breath-takers modified by the ice-blood would become even more impossible for humans. What really annoyed the scientists though was that no one had any idea where ice-blood came from. It was discovered by chance during a routine ice-harvest dig, with no clue as to who or what developed it or why it came to rest within our particular ice-glacier. These mysteries caused more arguments and clashes among the scientists and engineers than any notion of how to stop the Breath-takers from using the ice-blood to finish all humanity forever.

One such person had just finished setting up his experiment table, which shook during the sporadic bombing. Vadim, the lead engineer, who also liked to be called 'professor', moved his safety glasses in position and prepared to commence his experiment for the fifth time, only to be interrupted by a rather large bomb-quake. His eyes seemed to hold a gentle rebuke, as if to say: "How inopportune this bombing is today!"

Answering his look rather than his words I said: "Well, there's nothing we can do about it, can we? There's no crying over spilled bombs, you know".

This time Vadim did speak to me: "Nothing anyone could do? Crying over bombs as over spilled milk? It's not the same."

However, as much as he fussed over his experiment, yet another to try and identify the origin of the ice-blood, Vadim could do nothing against the Breath-taker bombing. Out of all the professionals, he was slightly more predisposed to care about finding a way of stopping the attacks. He was in fact more disturbed than I was over the attacks and was easily robbed of his sense of order and stability.

I, instead, looked for more practical matters and said in a voice loud enough to be heard by most of the group: "Why don't we shift our experiments into the basement? We could all work there, even going further underground if we need to."

In the face of growing murmurs from the team I emphasised the point: "Is it so hard to dig some more tunnels? We have plenty of drilling rigs, and now four working reactors to power them. Surely your research is worth the better protection!"

I was amazed that the group had listened to me this long – not a very common occurrence. I was even more amazed that Vadim immediately agreed to my plan and started to quickly pack away his equipment. Despite my idea, I was not exactly relishing the risk of a nuclear meltdown by performing necessary changes to the reactors to facilitate the move underground. Vadim would not be stopped though, he quickly did the rounds of the lab, instructing team members of the plan, until what seemed as a silly suggestion of mine turned into a mighty rescue operation.

The whole team worked without stopping for a whole Martian day. They moved tons of life support and technical equipment to the basement, and the drilling rigs were soon configured to bore new human accommodation. Through the work, I felt pleased that the reactors had behaved themselves during their power modification and hadn't done the Breath-taker's work for them by going critical at the wrong moment.

By the end of the move, the team seemed to be operating like robots themselves. Complex movement and thought seemed to have left them as they crashed down one by one on hastily prepared mattresses on the basement floor. Sometime that afternoon, I can't exactly remember when, my exhausted head finally found my small mattress and closed my eyes to sleep.

Sometime around midnight I came awake with a feeling that something was missing. My tired brain struggled to remember what it was. We had manhandled all the equipment down stairs, taking a careful inventory to make sure nothing important was left behind. Was it something else then?

Suddenly I remembered that Noosh was not with me! Thinking back, the last time I remember seeing my artificial pet was when I had taken down my mattress. I had told him to leave it alone as he was starting pecking the beads out of where I would need to put my head to rest. However, all thoughts of sleep left me as an abandoned base level would be no place for little Noosh, what with the bombings, or the ghost of a serial killer.

After climbing through what seemed endless stairs and bulkhead doors, I reached Level 2 of the Short Circuit Building. We had removed most of the power to this area, so everything was in total darkness. I was only able to see by my pocket torch. I moved slowly, as there were plenty of equipment connectors and loose cabling to trip over or run into. Something I didn't want to crash into was the serial killer – it seemed to be hiding just beyond every shadow or corner. Only my overwhelming desire to find my chicken kept me moving forward. Occasional flashes of stray electrical energy briefly lit up various circuits and light fixtures throughout the level as I kept searching, whispering Noosh's name.

The area was silent – with no power to run machinery. Even the bombing had stopped, leaving a noiseless void to get lost in. Following a dark corridor, I was strangely drawn to an oddly persistent series of electrical flashes. Unlike the other random flashes I had seen so far, these continued to come from the same source – an old cupboard. I found that very strange since no equipment was supposed to be stored inside this area. As I tried to look inside, I stumbled over something on the floor. They were safety goggles, of a type I had seen before. While trying to regain my balance, my right foot got trapped in their straps. I had to make a huge effort not to crash head first into the cupboard, I heard a faint noise coming from within. Finally regaining my balance, I listened again for the noise, preparing to run out fast if the serial killer did turn up. What sounded like a faint cry, followed by an electrical buzzing noise was definitely coming from inside. Finally overcoming my fears, I carefully opened the doors, and saw Noosh, or what was left of my pet. His head had been torn off, connected to the rest of the body by only a few wires. The artificial feathers, and lower legs were also a mess. The light I saw was coming up from Noosh's poor body attempting to maintain power to keep it active, and motion servos were still twitching.

Whoever had done this had tried to destroy the evidence, pulling out the chicken's eye sensors and main circuit boards, but Noosh's design was too sophisticated for that. Information and experiences were saved in many locations throughout his body in a neural net. I carefully gathered up the broken Noosh, putting him into discarded battery box. As I moved to return to the basement, my fear began to turn to rage – I didn't need Noosh to tell me who attacked him, or who the serial killer was.

Back in the basement the drilling rigs were making slow, steady progress. Their muffled noise wasn't enough to wake the team - most of them were still asleep on their mattresses, with the exception of the chief engineer. His bunk was empty. Our chief engineer, who was supposed to be leading our team, and researching new ways to defeat the Breath-takers, was gone, as I knew he would be. I lowered the basement lighting down a few notches, and moved to a corner to wait for his arrival.

Soon enough Vadim came quietly down the stairs, carefully closing the bulkhead door and looking pleased with himself that no one had noticed his absence, or so he thought. Just as his right foot touched the basement floor, I flashed the lighting full level while simultaneously shoving the safety glasses in his face.

"Forget something professor?" I said loudly enough for the whole team to hear, while also enjoying the moment as the chief engineer almost stumbled backwards over the stairs behind him. Trying to recover, he stammered out a story that he was looking for some gadgets to release the ice building pressure during the drilling. By this time many of the team members were waking up, partially from the bright lighting but also from our confrontation.

As our 'leader' continued to stammer out excuses for being absent, I twisted around and shoved the second item I carried under his nose; poor, broken Noosh.

"Care to explain this, serial killer?" I yelled at him. "And while you are at it, would you like to explain why you think destroying nuclear reactor service robots is such a good idea?"

One by one, other team members were slowly dawning to the truth behind the serial killer and why failure rates of life support machinery in the lab had been so high. Like the nuclear reactors that I had struggled so hard to repair and update, the destruction and subsequent lack of service robots had taken their toll on our equipment's critical reliability.

Vadim's eyes were like chips of ice as he hatefully replied "You and your monster robot! You know very well that they are killing us! If I don't act first, he would have killed you in your sleep!"

I was too disappointed to reply. After such a public confrontation our whole team were all disheartened for our professor to sink so low as to endanger our survival. Vadim was no war hero or scientific crusader, but simply the robot serial killer. A Breath-taker of flesh, little better than the enemy in orbit above.

What little credibility Vadim tried to regain with our team was lost forever when the reason behind the Breath-takers' cessation of bombing was eventually found. As the professor had been busy trying to kill Noosh, he had unwittingly transferred samples of ice blood from his contaminated tools onto the object of his rage. The amounts of ice-blood were microscopic, but were enough for Noosh's programming and abilities to exponentially evolve, and send a carrier stream signal to the Breath-takers orbiting above us. This communication, happening for only a few seconds, was enough to cycle the Breath-takers own programming. The signal reset the Breath-takers and shut down their receivers.

They were doomed to wait in standby for an activation signal that could never be received.

In the days that followed, Vadim, the once great warrior and scientist (at least in his eyes) had made his less-than gracious exit from our team for the last time, and was fast becoming a fading memory. Other team members, emboldened by the continued lack of activity from the Breath-takers, resumed their work on their research. Sadly, it was found that the ice-blood's unique properties were short lived. Noosh was the first and only major success of the ice-blood experiments, with all discovered samples decaying to inert compounds shortly afterward. As I began yet another round of nuclear reactor maintenance, unencumbered by the possibility of disappearing robots, I couldn't help but think that our lab had been saved not be warriors, or fantastic weapons, but by a robot chicken.

(Above) Noosh, the artificial chicken whose amateur construction and programming provided the key to shorten the second Bio War.

THE FALL

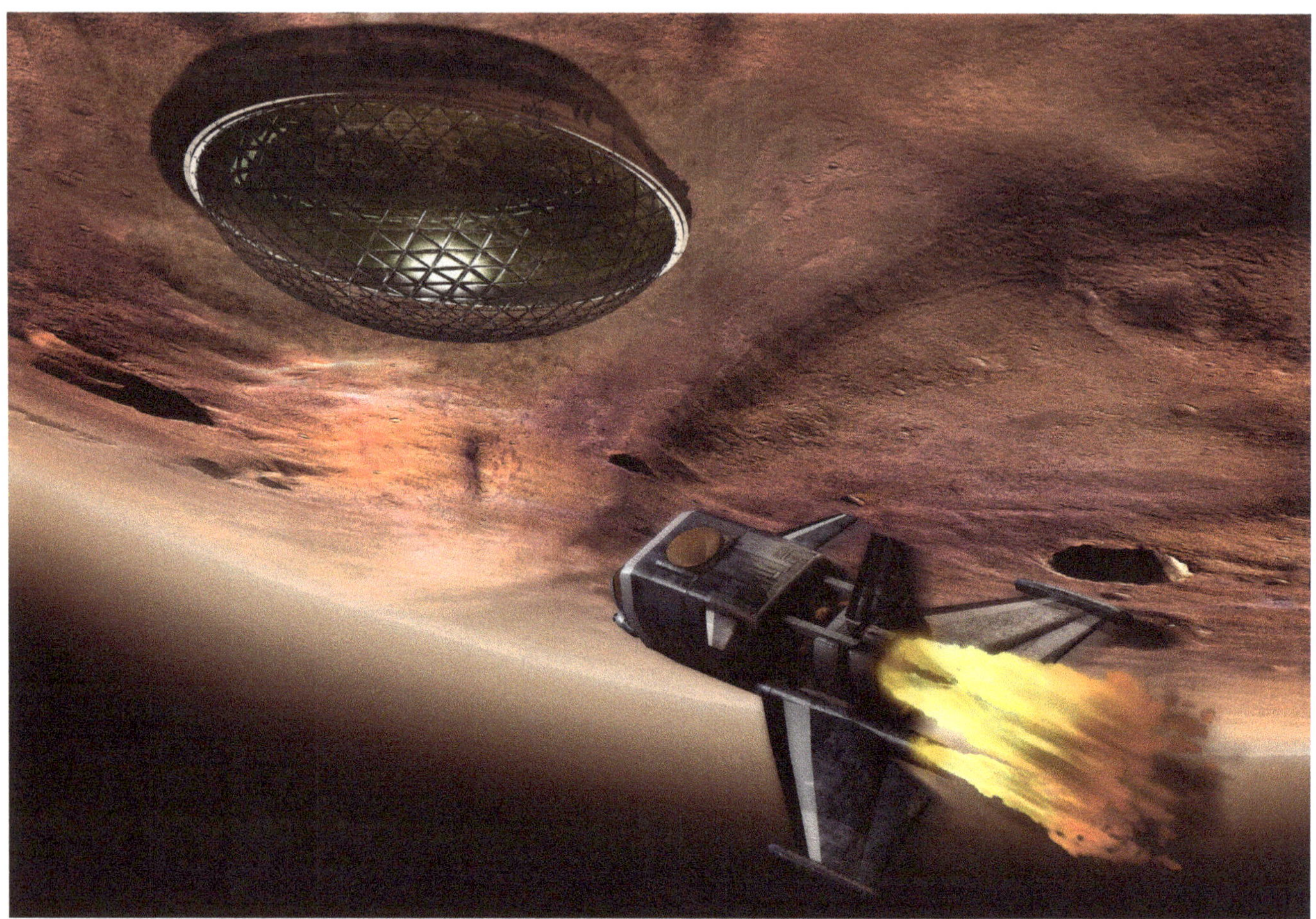

(Above) A shuttle damaged by space debris impacts spins out of control near Teera, a domed Mars habitat. Teera was one of a number of substantial colonies established on Mars following the Bio Wars.

The war with the Bions was meant to forever end society's experimentation with transhumanism, and for most of the generation that fought in that conflict, this was true. However, as the first explorers left their Earthly cradle for alien horizons, the mind set against artificially-sentient beings softened. The harsh reality of operating in the vacuum of space, plus a series of devastating accidents made convincing arguments in favour of robots in some quarters. People saw the benefit of having loyal companions that would be able to provide some mission assurance to crews - fragile flesh and blood creatures operating so far from home. Those working near Mars found the inert Breath-takers a ready source for constructing the next generation of 'helpers'. However, it was hard to argue this 'robotic companionship' case against those who had lost partners, parents or children to the Bio War.

'Bionics' soon featured a number of new crewed missions into the Solar System. Memories of the bitter past was were still fresh, and therefore suspicion of a second conflict launched from space began to develop back on Earth. Despite no supporting evidence, the mood eventually began to affect the human space explorers like those of the domed colonies established on Mars.

***

The noise of the spacecraft broke through the natural sounds of falling autumn leaves, the trademark of picturesque remote camp Teera. This camp was indeed very special for it was a tiny, unique colony - the first human nature reserve declared as 'a humani terraformania' or, in short, a terraformed environment of about 50 hectares on Mars. Teeran flowers had multiple medical usages, as well as great artistic value. It was almost unbelievable to even think that such an isolated oasis could be disrupted by noises other than those of nature.

The bang, followed by a small Martian quake, happened as the sun was fading and another dust storm was gathering outside the dome. Many heads preparing for night duties quickly popped out of several shelters to investigate. Looking up, they could not believe their eyes: a spacecraft was flying in drunken circles above the protective cover of the dome. A fragment had fallen off and struck the dome's roof – setting off all the alarms due to both sounding buzzes and irregular vibrations.

Although tired after a long day of work that involved maintaining the forest of plants, three dome inhabitants braced against the darkness and the coldness of the outside Martian world to go investigate the commotion. Ronny, the chief gardener, was the first to get out, followed by his assistant Dhea and her husband, Tanny. They were fascinated by the incoming noise and ground tremors. Once outside, Tanny tried to find a good position to watch the crashing shuttle, while reassuring his friends that the vehicle must have been lost since it was heading for an impact into their dome. The others initially thought this might be an attack from one of the conflicts arising out of the war with the breath-takers. Ronny convinced them that, apart from themselves, no-one thought their small colony was worth anything to anyone. Despite its exquisite gardens, the dome's infrastructure dated back to the initial colonisation, when numerous efforts of creating vast rainforests failed. So, most of their present equipment was obsolete by decades if not half a century. Teera was not even recorded on modern Martian maps. The inhabitants of this remote locality were quite happy to live unnoticed, in this enigmatic place configured by the nearby uniformly dusted and twisted Martian landscape.

"Without doubt the shuttle was in trouble before the impact," Ronny mumbled to himself as he watched the shuttle spin uncontrollably; the dome vibrated during its final noisy crash.

All three gardeners watched with horror as the wrecked machine began sliding swiftly down to the ground. After a few moments, the three of them noticed a pilot holding tight onto their harness as another occupant was catapulted out of the shuttle chair through the craft's motion down onto the Martian ground next to Gate 37. Purple flashes flickered at this gate, indicating that at least one of the passengers located outside the Teera perimeter was still alive despite the horrific crash. Dhea screamed and rushed to get to the gate first. Gate 37 was locked from the inside as it always was at nightfall. None of the group were quite ready to open it as per the established protocol. They changed their minds as the shuttle was heading into the Martian soil, and the two men reached the gate, put on their Mars suits and fiercely pushed against the emergency unlock hatch of Gate 37.

After an agonising wait of several minutes waiting for the pressure to equalise with the thin Martian air, they were confronted by a robotic-like creature spouting frightening flashes and sparks of short circuits throughout its body. Moments later, the second occupant, the one who had been thrown clear of the shuttle, thumped into the rust-red Martian soil a meter away from the first one. Looking much more human, with blood-red gashes to prove it, this second crash victim triggered an immediate response from the gardeners. With surprising speed and strength, they rushed the injured co-pilot through the gate into the dome where he began to gulp down life-giving Teera oxygen. The first survivor, still spouting the occasional flash of damaged electronics, was ignored by the rescue party.

The human survivor's eyes flicked open as his rescuers pulled him inside. He managed to utter some faint words: 'Be aware…The storm is coming. It brought down my Ginger…'

Dhea was shocked at the mention of 'Ginger' and its link to a distant past, as were the other two men. Isolated as they had been for decades, all of them had thought the Bionic War, with its Ginger squadron of paramilitary resistance fighters, was something long forgotten, almost a fantasy made up by people who were against progress. She then pointed to the crashed shuttle, smouldering outside the dome. Although greatly damaged from its fall to the ground, it still had a blue inscription: 'G for Ginger!'

The three rescuers, along with other arrivals, carefully took the injured man into the camp hospital and began to recover their senses after the immediate crisis had passed.

"Did this really happen – a shuttle blown out of the sky by Bions? Are we under attack by robots?" shrieked a worried Dhea.

"This Ginger member might have not survived if it hadn't been for our dome!" said Ronny.

An otherwise unresponsive Tanny nodded in agreement. "And to see a real Bionic at our doorstep! What does this mean?! Is this the end of our gardens?" said Dhea as she remembered the presence of the first creature from the shuttle crash.

Forgotten until now, the presence of the damaged being, not quite human and not quite robot, standing resolutely in front of Gate 37, was brought back to the groups' collective attention.

"Oh, no, we've worked these fields for generations, I'm not about to be moved now!" an optimistic husband replied, though not without fear.

"Well let's make sure the one Bion we actually know about is no longer functioning. It looked pretty beat up from the crash', said Ronny encouraging them to follow him once more outside the Teera dome.

At once the small group moved to Gate 37 to go outside to the damaged shuttle and look for the first survivor. Entering the airlock, they carefully peered through the thick window at the crash site. There was no Bionic in sight, only the damaged shuttle partially buried in the Martian dust. Tanny shrieked while Dhea reminded the guys that the soft drifts of dust surrounding Teera might have slowed the spacecraft's impact with the ground enough for the human co-pilot to survive.

The notable absence of the second shuttle occupant shook the group. Was it hiding under cover, ready to ambush and slaughter them as they ventured outside? Tanny broke, reaching for the gate abort switch: "It's gone - disappeared! Let's get out of here!" he blurted out, Panic-stricken.

Ronny's gloved hand firmly grasped Tanny by the shoulder, spinning him around. "Relax, it has probably fried all its circuits from the crash and crawled under of the shuttle to expire. Instead of looking for it, let's just seal the gate and make sure the security video system is working here."

"We've had enough for today," agreed Dhea.

The trio in the airlock had turned their backs to the crash site. They did not see the subtle movement of the shuttle wreck. This movement also went unobserved by the Teera video surveillance system that, due to the groups haste in exiting the gate, was not properly activated. So, they all got inside inserting the required code, which was quickly scanned by the hidden Bionic's one working eye.

Tihia7003, the pilot of the 'G for Ginger' craft, was specialised in planetary defence. She was designed to recognise incoming meteors and destroy them before they came too close to Mars. This latest meteor incursion proved too hard to stop. Now too damaged to progress her task, Tihia7003 hoped the nearby colony could be evacuated in time.

The night came to an abrupt end while Tihia7003 was still self-repairing her damaged circuits. After the crash, not quite restored, she slowly peered out from underneath the wreckage. She wanted to find

(Above) The artificial environment of Teera was able to support a substantial ecosystem. This also included substantial bodies of standing water.

her captain. He needed to know that the humans considered her as a threat, that they thought she was the one responsible for hitting the dome, not an asteroid.

Sneaking inside the dome, her sensors picked up no hospital activity and there was no way she could continue her search during the day unnoticed. So, as the blue dawn made way for a salmon pink day, she decided to stay put in her small hiding place: a big supply box.

The three colonists eventually forgot about the Bionic threat as the distractions of the new day occupied their attention. They continued their work in the nursery where the small seeds were growing well, even in the six-month long Martian autumn. They planned to visit the injured captain at lunchtime to see how he was coping, but their busy schedule pushed that meeting too late into the evening and then, to their disappointment, their patient was fast asleep.

During that first night, the Bionic had felt very lonely; deciding on the spot to come out of her hiding spot and look for her colleague. Tihia7003 found enough gardening utensils to disguise herself as a colonist. It didn't take her long to know where the field hospital was and she felt confident that she could easily scan for signs of where the last patient might be located. Observing worried expressions of the medics coming in or out of a particular room, as if the team was dealing with a guest of some importance, narrowed her search.

The Bionic stepped inside the room and scanned the face of the man lying there. When she had no doubt that the man was Captain Ricky Tulbot, she quickly hid under her boss' bed. There might still be a way to warn what was about to hit that colony, she hoped.

When the shrunken sun rose again in the Martian sky, Tihia7003 heard sharp noises as if someone was grinding stones. She told herself that this could be part of some medical experiment the humans were about to test on her boss. While not happy about it, she knew she could do nothing, so she tried to distract herself by scanning the room and all the medical staff that came inside the room.

At midday she noticed the three humans who had brought her captain in arrive. She read mistrust on their bodies. Dhea spoke: "What if this fellow willingly came here to make sure that our colony gets involved in this war once we have suffered of the hands of his Bionic colleague?"

"Nonsense, Dhea. He had no choice. He was probably not aware that the robot was even inside his shuttle. The Bionics are like that, you know. We can't predict what they are going to do next and there is no way we are going to win if we get involved in such war," replied Ronny.

"True, staying hidden and ignoring calls for help is our best chance of surviving," confessed a reluctant Tanny.

"Yes, it always works. Let's hope this accident was random and not a planned assault," agreed an optimist Dhea.

Tihia7003 almost wished that their shuttle had made a crack in these arrogant people's dome. Maybe she had 'a conscience' like humans call it; she didn't know. As a Bionic, she was happy she was able to keep her friendships with humans. They made her who she was and she liked to think that all Bionics were unique like her. Her and Ricky, the captain, were a team. Just two days ago were ready to let others know that if Bionics and humans didn't work together, this part of Mars would soon be an asteroid crater.

As she saw the trio leave, she stood up and touched Ricky's chest: "Hey, captain, it's time to get up!"

To her unbelief, her boss opened his eyes, looked at her and smiled. She told him that they both should talk to the colonists about the impending asteroid event threatening the colony. She told him that she would help him with the task when the next nurse came to check on him, to which Ricky nodded weakly.

However, the unexpected happened: while she lay under the bed, doctors came in and moved Ricky into another room. Their plan had to wait. It was vital for Ricky to have Tihia7003 next to him when he explained the meteor threat to the colonists. It was her brain that had scanned and memorised the incoming asteroid formation, including the maneuverers able to deflect teach one of them. The Bionic was the key to preventing a catastrophe, but the humans didn't trust her.

What could she do? It was too risky for her to try to find Ricky again…she would have to confront the three colonists herself when they were back doing their 'mercy round'. She knew it would be hard to try to reason with them, but she had no choice.

So, when Tihia7003 heard footsteps beating a rhythm that her AI recognised, she moved out of her hiding place and tried to look as friendly as possible. Dhea and the man next to her reacted first by fainting, while slightly later her husband pulled out an electric gun, pointing it at the Bionic. Tihia had no choice but to hit the man with the gun, making Ronny jump with fear. She tried to explain the reason why she and Ricky were there, but all Ronny was doing was staring at her and whispering: "This is not real; this is not happening to me; this must end soon."

The bionic had enough; she then hit him hard, almost breaking his neck but making him look straight at her.

"Stop it, you fool! I am not your enemy! We are here because you are all going to die soon unless you use your small brains and listen to me!"

When she realised that she had his full attention, she once again started explaining that she wasn't the real enemy, but a friend, ready to help their colony survive the asteroid storm due to start the next day. She asked for her captain and Ronny took her down the hallway.

The rallying Ricky sat straight up in his bed. He added his agreement to Tihia7003's words. Seeing that he was not about to die that instant, Ronny started to relax and then appeared to go along with their story. Then, with excessive head and hand gestures he apologised for the misunderstanding and promised to notify the Colony's commander of the danger. Shaking of his head and waving of arms to state his agreement, Ricky signalled thumbs up to a worried Tihia.

Leaving his companions behind, Ronny ran straight for the nearest security guards. When he met two officers, he blurted out his story so fast that he was almost unintelligible. The guards half heard Ronny's rant about a shuttle captain and a Bionic, and the imminent conspiracy about to kill all colonists as part of some hideous plan.

At hearing the word 'bionic', the colour drained from the guards' faces. They were petrified; the extent of their combat experience was trying to stop crazy scientists doing stupidly unsafe things. To have an actual Bionic collaborating with a master human criminal in the colony was a whole new level.

Ronny had spoken so loudly that other colonists had converged on the scene, including more guards. The group came up with some sort of plan where a master SOS signal would be sent to get help, while the bravest of the group set out for the recovery area to apprehend the captain and Bionic. To Ronny's disbelief, they rushed headlong, hoping that their weight of numbers would be enough to overpower the strange pair. Rounding the corridor, the crowd burst through the door, makeshift weapons raised, and knocked over Dea and Tanny, who had just recovered and were sitting on the otherwise empty hospital bed.

At that moment, Ricky and Tihia2003 were skimming across the surface of Mars in a stolen land craft. Ronny had spoken so loudly during his encounter with the guards that the Bionic's sensitive hearing alerted them to the dangers. With the bionic half-carrying Ricky, they had both fled, taking the first available transport to get outside the danger zone.

Following the discovery of the empty hospital room, the momentum of the crowd suddenly dissipated. The urgency seemed to have passed, and the Teera botanists and even security guards were keener to return to their normal routines rather than try to chase potentially dangerous fugitives across the Martian desert. Even the discovery of a small storage device that would have shown critical details of the asteroid strike had anyone decided to examine its contents failed to generate much interest. Dhea and Tanny decided the best form of recovery was to tend to their plants and prepare them for the approaching night. Ronny had retreated to his quarters to try to write up the events of the last two days, including how to explain the SOS that was now cancelled. A detail of security guards was outside. There were notionally preparing to dispose of the crashed lander but really admiring the beautiful blue twilight as the Martian sun set on Teera for the final time.

THE PYRAMIDS OF MARS

(Above) The Martian Pyramids rise out of early morning fog. They easily dwarfed the Mars exploration rover sent to investigate them. The corrosive Martian dust forced explorers to use a medication nicknamed 'The Choke' to maintain their health.

Sandra started coughing for the third time in the comfortably cramped rover. Pressurised to a relaxed shirtsleeve environment, Martian dust seemed to find a way to invade this sheltered environment.

"You need to do the choke," Karnik briefly glanced away from the driver controls to look at his companion as he advised his colleague on the private comms channel. Both Karnik and Sandra were in their Mars suits but without helmets. Being partially suited saved time when it meant going outside into the thin environment.

"I'm fine," Sandra shot back between coughs. "Why don't you concentrate on driving so we don't run into a sand dune?"

Sandra was one of the most experienced Martians, having clocked up thousands of hours of Mars walks. She also had a firm hand in re-invigorating the pure form of exploration following the chaotic post-Bio War period, though the accumulated exposure to Martian dust was starting to take its toll.

A second bout of coughing caused Karnik to make an excuse to mission control and stop the rover temporarily. "Look, I've bought us a few minutes and turned off the com. Let's do the choke together – it won't be so bad."

Sandra frowned, but inwardly knew Karnik was right. In a way she liked him; new but with the attitude of a future mission commander. Resigning herself to her fate, she helped Karnik with the "Respiratory Maintenance medicine," scornfully called the choke by those forced to use it.

Karnik counted three, they both inhaled the pleasant tasting medicine, then promptly had dry retching fits.

Panting after the attack that had ended as quickly as it begun, Karnik prudently eased the rover back onto its course before Sandra could say something nasty. As unpleasant as the choke was, the crafted medicine caused the body to violently eject Martian dust from the respiratory system, preventing debilitating 'red lung disease' from inhalation of Martian dust.

Trying to lighten the mood, Karnik asked: "So do you think these formations we're going to are actually Martian pyramids? I have heard the conspiracy theorists are going nuts over the aerial surveys of these things."

"The mathematical analysis showed a regular four-sided structure, and their shadows are consistent with built structures," a recovering Sandra answered.

Just then the outside coms link came to life: "Wheels one, we have you almost at the top of the hill, your first waypoint. You should get a good look into the valley from there."

Sandra responded: "Wheels one, Roger. Going has been a little slow from the landscape changes caused by the most recent storm. Here's hoping we can get to the bottom of those pre-war legends."

Karnik keyed the mike: "Wheels one cresting the hill now, we're just getting a view of the valley now. We are a bit late and the sun is in our eyes but…"

"Wheels one, control here. You cut off there. Repeat your last for the folks back home."

The communications silence from Wheels One, the rover team, began to stretch uncomfortably. Calls from mission control became more insistent, as fears of an accident with the rover team began to be considered.

In reality the cause for the communication break was more prosaic. Karnik and Sandra, coming face to face with clear evidence of artificial construction on the surface of Mars, were simply staring stunned, their mission forgotten. Two tetrahedral structures towered 70 metres above the red sands, built from interlocking plates of basaltic rock.

The first two humans to confirm the existence of extra-terrestrial artifacts were joined by a small army of explorers over the coming weeks. Using the latest sensors and tools, they fed data into a growing mass of professionals who theorised, and philosophised as to what the pyramids were and who built them. Scurrying from one end of the site to the other was Sandra, trying her best to keep over-enthusiastic scientists safely on mission. Striding past one group of ground radar specialists, she caught a familiar face moving toward her.

The sight of Karnik brought a smile to Sandra, which deepened as he signed that they change to a private communications channel.

"So what has brought you out to here again Karnik, come to check up on us?" Sandra asked on the private channel.

"Everyone thinks you are doing a great job," Karnik replied, "and of course Mission Control and just about everyone else are busting for news of extra discoveries."

"I bet they are," Sandra said." We certainly have enough staff out here – it's a full-time job trying to make sure they don't do anything stupid. Can you believe one of them jumped outside without a glove

The discovery of ruins on Mars prompted unprecedented levels of exploration. The ruins also provided clues to an ancient civilisation inhabiting the Red Planet.

(Above) Violent Martian dust storms exposed additional ruins in the Martian desert. Most were located near what appeared to be shorelines of shallow lakes. Evidence of damage from forces other than natural decay were also found at the sites.

seal done up? We had to shut down a whole airlock for hours so the med team could help him.”

Karnik grinned inside his helmet. “If it's any consolation, some of my scientists might have been told to do the choke four times more than was actually needed. It's hard to be arrogant and condescending when you spend half your base time in the recovery position.”

Sandra laughed at the image of vastly intelligent academics doubled over in an uncomfortable, but entirely harmless position. “So, what are you really here for then?”

“I just wanted to give you a heads up that Mission Control are planning a high-level media conference on the Pyramids, and of course they want off-the-cuff, expert opinions from you as the site lead.”

Sandra groaned. “I suspected as much. I don't know what more to tell them than what they already know.”

“Which is...?” Karnik prompted.

“Well, that the Pyramids' outer construction is made of interlocking basaltic rock that covers a hardened inner structure that defies penetration from our radar or drilling rigs, and that they are practically identical. Did I miss anything?”

Karnik was about to reply when their suit visor displays flashed a priority emergency message. They both hastily switched to the public channel, with Sandra fervently hoping someone had not accidentally popped their helmet off.

"…Repeat, priority alpha message, severe storm warning. Abort all outdoor activities, and retreat to the nearest shelter…"

Karin and Sandra lost themselves in the professional chaos that followed. Surprisingly, none of the scientists protested, and were too happy to be shepherded back through the airlocks as the sky began to visibly darken. Sandra, the last to leave the site, took one last look back at the pyramids, hoping that she would get another chance to investigate them again after the storm had passed.

The dust storm season was particularly violent that year, with tons of regolith being moved by powerful winds. Sandra and her team were grounded for weeks, writing up findings and generally waiting for the storm to subside. South of her location, one of the few Martian pilots was also waiting out the global storm raging in his area. Quietly fuming at lost flight time, Nathan Davis had no idea that he and Sandra would come together for a live interview over another profound discovery of artificial ruins in the cold Martian sands.

Interviewer: "Welcome to our program. Since the Martian Pyramids have become so popular in our folklore, what we want to explore in this edition is whether this latest discovery of a ruined city has any relation to the pyramids of Mars."

Co-host: "That's right. These ruins were just discovered by Nathan Davis, remote pilot from the 400 strong Martian base situated near Hellas Basin.

Interviewer: "Nathan, how did you come across the ruins of an ancient city on Mars? Try to explain the experience in detail to our viewers."

Nathan: "My position at the time was a field pilot. This meant that I was responsible for the transportation of supplies and people from base to base, and to and from orbit. Sometimes, when the usual remote probes and satellites were unavailable, we would use our aircraft for limited mapping exercises."

Co-host: "Am I correct that the satellites were down because you were experiencing one of the worst dust storms on record? I remember some apprehension back on Earth."

Nathan: "That's correct. It was certainly coming closer to the base I was operating from. It was so bad in certain places that some areas had to be evacuated. The rest of us were confined underground. Nothing outside except for a swirling murky light was visible outside the windows.

Interviewer: "Evacuation? Was it really that bad?"

Nathan: "It was. In fact, when the storm finally subsided and it was safe to leave the base, we needed to assess how much the landscape had changed during the storm. As you could imagine, huge amounts of land had been shifted and most of our previous maps were next to useless. The storm had also affected our remote sensing systems, so the pilots were given the task of initial mapping until orbital resources were brought back online."

Interviewer: "Tell us about the discovery."

Nathan: "Two days after the storm passed, I was on a mapping run over Acidalia when I just happened to look straight down. I noticed what looked like slim spires sticking out of the landscape. At first, I thought I was off course and that I had accidently flown over another base, but when I checked my position, I found that I was where I was supposed to be. I radioed base control about my sighting, and I was given permission to investigate further.

As I drew closer to the position of the sighting, it looked less and less like one of our bases. At that stage, I had a couple of cameras on the thing so that the control team was able to see what I was looking at. And since we were all pretty excited, I pushed my plane to its operational limit to get the best possible views.”

Interviewer: “Can you describe what you saw?”

Nathan: “The structures themselves were half buried in the sand and were of varying height, the highest being maybe 50 meters. They were made out of this grey material that looked like either metal or plastic, I couldn’t say for sure. From the exterior, everything looked fairly badly corroded, falling apart and about to tumble. I think that the ruins of this city must have been there for a very long time.”

Co-host: “Thank you Nathan. We’ll cross now to Professor Sandra Watt, one of the most renowned archaeologists of our time. She is leading the on-ground investigation of the ruins.”

Sandra: “Like the Pyramids of Mars, we haven’t discovered a lot about the origins or formation of this ancient city. At least not yet. What we can say is that its builders might not have been too different from ourselves in regard to their physiological makeup.”

Interviewer: “That’s amazing! How could you possibly know that?”

Sandra: “We inferred this by studying the ruins’ structure. The entrances and accesses of the buildings’ interiors were most suitable for something of approximately human proportions. Stairs have also been found in many structures that are most easily crossed by something that has similar strides to the average human adult. If you put all these pieces of information together, you see that the city was built by either humans or a species close to humans.”

Co-host: “Professor, where do you think these builders came from? Might they be the same builders as the Pyramids?”

Sandra: “Unfortunately we don’t know where these beings come from or where they went. The structures themselves have several similarities to the Pyramids of Mars, though the materials used are completely different. We believe that these two large artefacts share a common origin and were possibly even built by the same species. This is our current hypothesis, and we hope that further evidence proves it further, or at least gives us more answers.”

Interviewer: “Is there anything else you can tell us about the ruins?”

Sandra: “The ruins also differ from the Pyramids because the builders, for some reason, must have thought that there was no reason to properly guard the interiors of the buildings from us. We hoped that the act of entering these buildings would uncover great information about their history. However, the interiors of these buildings we have explored so far were stripped of everything, leaving behind bare floors and walls. We still haven’t uncovered any artefacts. As such we can assume that the city was abandoned and stripped soon afterwards, leaving empty shells behind. Unfortunately, the reason why this had happened remains also unknown.”

Co-host: “How old are these ruins? Could they possibly be from an old colony before the Bio Wars??

Sandra: “Almost certainly not. These ruins are very old, judging from their advanced structure and degree of decay. Our team has become convinced that the city was built around 5,000 years ago, and assuming that the corrosion we see is entirely due to the Martian climate, I also think this is a reasonable estimate.”

Interviewer: “We have had reports that these ruins might point to a more hospitable period on Mars. What do you think?”

Sandra: “After studying the buildings’ structures and exploring the degree of their decay, we believe that the city was not built for the current climate. The construction of the buildings is too flimsy to hold a pressurised atmosphere that would have been needed to support oxygen-breathing life."

Co-host: "Thanks for your reports Professor. We also have Dr Igor Reiss, senior astrobiologist with us. Dr Reiss, I understand that you have made some discoveries that might help unravel the mysteries of Mars?"

Igor: "I don't know about solving great mysteries, and my discoveries don't quite compare with ruined cities."

Interviewer: "I understand they are important discoveries though. Can you tell us about them?"

Igor: This mudstone I'm holding up now came from the floor of Valles Marineris behind me. If you look closely you can see clear evidence of fossilised plants. This, of course, suggests that Mars once had an Earth-like climate."

Interviewer: "Thank you all for a wonderful time. One last question to you Professor Watt, where to next?"

Sandra: "If we could simply make contact or find the remnants of the species who built these ruins, then we might understand more. However, my personal belief is that the race who once lived on Mars left before whatever caused Mars to become the harsh climate it is now. All of us here are trying to work out where next to start looking."

(Above) One of a number of geology survey rovers rests near mummified shellfish discovered in a dried Martian lake bed. This and other artifacts were found above much drier geological layers, leading researchers to believe that Mars had once been terraformed in the distant past.

THE KANE WARP DRIVE

(Above) Images such as this were used to sell the idea of interstellar travel to enthusiastic explorers. Faster than light travel was made possible through the invention of the Kane Warp Drive.

"Are you comfortable Chancellor Kane?" The flight crew asked.

The frail old man to whom the question was addressed smiled inwardly to himself. He thought 'chancellor' had a nice ring to it. A fitting end for decades of service and one final contribution to space exploration.

To the crew member he simply replied: "Yes thank you, I'm fine."

In truth, now-Chancellor Kane was not fine. He had lived well past his allotted years, and this trip to the outer Solar System had almost killed him. Kane fully expected not surviving the return journey, and at his request the team he was with was prepared to conduct a deep space burial of his body, should the need arise.

"Twenty minutes until fly-past," announced an overhead voice.

At this call, the media representative—Ava, Kane thought her name was—began pestering the long-retired manager with her questions.

"Sorry to disturb you again, Chancellor, I just would like to make sure we are all set for the main event.”

Rylee, Kane's executive assistant, seeing the subtle look of pain on her aging boss's face, broke off her side conversation and hurried to his side.

“Excuse me, Ava, I'm sure you would want Chancellor Kane well rested before the main event. Perhaps I can help provide you with what you need to know.”

Sensing the rescue, Chancellor Kane shuffled away as fast as his old legs could take him. In the meantime, Rylee told the story he had shared hundreds of times.

“The Pyramids of Mars convinced us that there was life outside of their own home world. However, spacecraft still had to travel larger distances to reach their next destination, and it took years to simply receive data from them. Chancellor Kane headed one of the largest scientific and engineering endeavours in human history to find out how to travel faster than light. Starting decades ago, the project was given a boost from technology found on Mars.”

Ava interrupted as the overhead system announced the ten minute mark: “How does it actually work?”

Kane, having shuffled back to the conversation, could not help but interject, reliving the discovery once more. “The device works by creating a field around an object. This would allow anything within that warp to leave its current space-time continuum and travel through the field. Once the field ended, the object would then drop back into the universe but at a different position from where it first started.”

Ava began to understand. “Under these specific circumstances, the Kane Warp Drive could cause an object to travel faster than the speed of light. But was there not a problem in that the final position of the object would be unpredictable, meaning it could end up anywhere?”

“Yes,” the old man said. “More work had to be done through sending numerous unmanned probes throughout space to track their positions before and after the usage of the Drive. We then fed the data to massive computers which then modeled and mapped possible destinations to some degree of accuracy. This took years, before we could get the maps good enough to be safe.”

“Five minutes until fly-past”.

“One last question if I may Chancellor,” Ava said. “How does it feel to be here to finally see the first crewed mission use your warp drive to travel to Alpha Centauri, Earth's nearest star?”

Kane paused for a long moment, thinking through the decades of research, culminating in this moment. He also couldn't help but remember the friends and colleagues of his team he had lost trying to handle forces too exotic for standard physics. One of his sons was among them. Coming out of his reflection, he simply said: “It is an honour to be here, and I wish the crew of Kane 3 all the very best in their pioneering adventure.”

“Two minutes until fly-past.”

Hurriedly thanking Kane for his time, Ava suddenly moved to introduce the fly-past to her virtual viewers.

“In less than two minutes from now, twenty astronauts are undertaking the most historic journey since the first Moon landings. After months of planning and training, the Kane 3's enormous rocket engines roared to life. Leaving the orbit of Uranus, their spacecraft has kept accelerating to over one hundredth the speed of light for a period of 20 days.

“Seconds from now, they will pass our position near Neptune and activate the Kane Warp Drive, becoming the first humans to officially leave the Solar System. Travelling to Earth's nearest star, Proxima Centauri, they will run as many tests as possible to learn more about the new system. There is also great excitement in the hope that this mission might find evidence of extrasolar life.”

The first evidence of intelligent life outside our Solar System was discovered resting in a geothermal lake on a Moon of Herculis.

"Fly-past imminent."

Ava and all non-essential members crowded around the windows. A comet-like streak appeared, moving at a ridiculous speed. Collective breaths were held as the time came for Kane Warp Drive activation. Everyone imagined what it must have looked like aboard that spacecraft, speeding through space. They imagined the craft's glowing exterior as it violated conventional laws of physics.

On Kane 3, twenty astronauts prepared for the most hazardous part of the journey. Twenty percent of the spaceship's total energy resources were suddenly pumped into the warp drive and soon the universal balance was broken. Kane squinted as his namesake seemed to explode in rays of oranges and white. It was as if the very fabric of the universe was torn as the ship disappeared from view.

At that instant, all communication feeds between Kane 3 and the known universe halted, promptly vanishing with the spacecraft. All that was left was the blackness of space, and an old man, turning his face from the light so no one could see his tears.

Four months later, Executive assistant, now general Director, Rylee once again faced Ava and her virtual audience. The passing of her mentor and friend softened the otherwise good news she was about to share with Ava.

"They made it," she said in answer to Ava's question. She imagined a miniature supernova appearing in the orbit of a gas planet within the Proxima Centauri region, from which the cold grey lines of the first interstellar traveller emerged. The Kane Warp Drive had worked! After course corrections were made, the craft successfully entered the orbit of the Proxima planet and transmitted its presence to the anxious controllers on Earth via a near-instantaneous communication system designed by the Kane team.

"As we speak, robotic probes are sampling Proxima b's atmosphere to prepare for the crewed landings scheduled next week. They will have a busy time ahead of them, collecting, sampling, testing and photographing what they could in the short time available. Back home we will have our work ahead of us, analyzing the enormous quantity of data gathered and sent back home for the experts to pore over and interpret what the astronauts saw."

"I have heard that the Kane 3 mission suffered some malfunctions and are having to cut their mission short," Ava said. "How long do they actually have at Proxima?"

Rylee tried not to get too defensive. "As you know, safety is our number one priority. We have had to cut the science short to the bare essentials. They will commence their return journey at an earlier window, 11 days from now."

Too soon the inevitable window of opportunity for return to Earth arrived, and all aboard knew that the consequences of missing it would be disastrous. Return trajectories were calculated, and the Kane Warp Drive was reactivated to bring the mission safely back home. While the safe return of Kane 3 was celebrated, the search for extrasolar life would have to wait.

The success of the Proxima exploration caused many more missions to take place, and soon a kind of star race was once again formed. A staging point near Neptune rapidly developed to fuel thirsty interstellar spacecraft. Eventually a whole Kuiper Belt mining industry gained momentum, with many risking the dangers for lucrative profits. Many countries also attempted to own the Kane technology exclusively in order to gain an exploration advantage, and spacecraft pushed the frontiers ever further.

Shortly afterwards, a friendly, though aggressive, competition arose among the different space agencies to see who would be the first to find evidence of a past or current civilization situated beyond our home world. This was unexpectedly won by the Southern Exploratory Team, who had sent a mission to the system of Herculis, nearly 60 light years away from Earth.

The Southern team set up orbit around the Herculis b gas giant, investigating several of its moons in various orbits. On one of these moons the team made a discovery that shocked the world for decades to come.

The exploratory phase of the Herculis System had reached an advanced stage, with ultra-detailed mapping a high priority. As an orbital camera was surveying a moon belonging to the gas planet, it spotted a formation on its surface that seemed out of place compared to everything else. However, the camera had insufficient resolution to resolve anything further. Geographers and scientists speculated over what it was as they began examining the scene. Perhaps a patch of ice or a mere rock that caught the Herculis star reflection?

An EVA team was dispatched to the area for a closer look. As they drew closer, they realised what they were looking at: it was a derelict spacecraft. The holes in the structure's decaying side implied that the craft was of extreme age.

Once permission was granted, the astronauts carefully climbed into the dead spacecraft through a large hole. Lamps were lit to reveal empty hallways within the dark interior. Wires and conduits hung above their heads, some resting on shelves and others attached to bulkheads.

Further down one of the gloomy corridors, a door had been wrenched off and only hung by one hinge. The astronauts found that it led to a smaller room that was in better condition than the rest of the ship. One particular find riveted their attention: amongst scattered debris and remains of a pressurised suit lay a human skeleton!

The idea of finding something like this in a solar system apart from their own was simply preposterous. Yet, there was a yellow, decaying body which seemed to grin back at the explorers in defiance. Since the astronauts making this discovery didn't have the proper equipment for the examination and the removal of the body, the world had to wait until a team of anthropologists was transported to the lonely spot. Once they arrived, the body was carefully removed and taken to a quarantine facility to undergo rigorous safety and deep biological analysis tests.

Soon tests came back: the skeleton belonged to an adult male around the age of 35-45 years. He stood 1.74 metres tall and weighed approximately 72 kilograms. The man had short brown hair, some of which was found near his body. As far as the scientists could tell, there was no disability or ailment that could have caused his death. That was where the facts about this man stopped. No other data could be obtained from the current remains and the specialists were forced to give intelligent guesses at the numerous questions posed to them by the public. The questions came at them like missiles. What did the man die of? Did humanity achieve space travel earlier in history? Where did he come from? Are there any other artifacts to be found on other worlds? What happened to the rest of his crew? Did this finding bear any relation to the artifacts found on Mars, which even now defied analysis despite careful scrutiny?

Further analysis showed similarities between the ruins on Mars and this spacecraft. Perhaps those who built the Pyramids of Mars and the red planet's ruins were also the people who sent this lone man to that lonely moon. Many theories were put forward to explain the disappearance of this mysterious race, all ranging from disease to war. Whether any of these were true, there was not yet any way to know.

THE UNUSUAL SUSPECT

(Above) An interstellar explorer gazes with interest at a Triton volatile mining site. At this altitude, the poor work standards that accompanied operations such as this were impossible to see. Most travellers were only too eager to reach their destination with little thought of the cost of getting there.

"Welcome to Neptune, last Solar System outpost before interstellar space!" chimed an enthusiastic flight-host announcement.

"Our flight will lay over briefly to take on fresh supplies before our interstellar journey," the announcement continued. "In the meantime, the cabin lights will be dimmed so you can take full advantage of the panoramas that the Neptune system has to offer."

Ivan was one of the older passengers making this interstellar flight, now becoming much more routine since the first Proxima Centauri mission. As the lights went down, he lost himself in the aqua blue light of Neptune, and the bright star field, of which the Sun was just a brighter spark. He could not see, but only imagine, the tons of ice-rich material brought in from Triton and the Kuiper Belt to feed hungry Kane warp drive engines.

Suddenly he turned to the passenger sitting beside him. "They say that the Kuiper zone is haunted."

The younger man pulled his attention away from his work – business work, Ivan thought, and gave his fellow passenger an incredulous look.

"It's true!" insisted Ivan. "They say a lonely soul wanders endlessly between frozen comets, searching for something that can never be found."

"Really? In these times of interstellar travel?" countered the young man. "What could possibly be out there that is worth haunting? I understand almost all resource mining done out here is pretty much mechanised and automated."

"It may be so now, but that wasn't always the case," said one of the flight customer service staff who, like the passengers, had some time while waiting for the flight to be underway again.

"Years ago, most of the Neptune station had to be prepared and operated by hand, and it was these remote surveys to the Kuiper belt that came back with the ghost stories."

"Recordings of strange movement, something jumping between the ice bodies, mysterious breakdowns and disappearances of the early mining robots," the older man said, encouraged.

The businessman was unmoved. "Grainy recordings on obsolete sensors that could have easily been radiation noise, and robots disappearing? I thought that would have happened all the time back then." To him, this closed the discussion. He had work to do, no ghosts need apply. He closed his mind to stories he heard years ago; of veterans who worked the Kuiper Belt, and how the movement seen out of the corner of the eye, and mysterious breakdowns had been too much for many of them. Very few returned miners talked about it, not even now.

Forty years previously, an ice crusher was having trouble staying on its harvest track on Triton. The controller fighting the machine had been hard at it for nearly 60 hours. Often, he would work past 200 hours at a stretch, but the harvester was obviously broken and he was grateful for a break.

The controller called in an unscheduled stoppage and, working deftly, had isolated and removed the faulty subsystem, and bounced along with it in Triton's low gravity to the base.

Inside the pressurised workshop dome that also doubled as equipment storage, headquarters, food hall and sleeping quarters, the controller placed the subsystem in the diagnostics cradle, He had just started the equipment when suddenly he was moving sideways, arcing through the bay before crashing against heavy mining equipment.

"So, you've come to take our breaths, Stitch?" cried Lucas, who had just sent the controller reeling by a heavy blow of his Boltzmann rifle's butt.

Two more miners came into the base, following the noise.
"Bions, Breath-takers, you wait until we are asleep and then try to come here to start another war," said Rhett, the nearest of the miners who had joined Lucas.

"The ice crusher has a fault. I'm trying to fix it. I called it in…" said the controller before another butt stroke slammed his head against the floor.

"We heard nothing," said Lucas, cocking the double chambers of the Boltzmann. "Time to finish what the Foxhound started, Stitch."

It was Lucas's turn to do a graceful low-gravity arc as his Boltzmann was wrested from his grip by two strong metallic arms.

"Leave him alone!" screamed Giana, the newcomer. "The reason you didn't get the signal is because you have the receiver turned off, again."

"Sure, stand up for the Bion, Halfer." Sneered Lucas as the other miners slowly advanced. "So which half of you is on Stitches' side? The human half or your bionic half? You get less human by the day."

The servos in Giana's artificial arms whined as she prepared to do her best to merge Lucas's Boltzmann with his head. She was interrupted by a concussive shock that temporarily disoriented the group.

"So, what are you all doing here and why has my harvester stopped?" said Damon, the mining chief.

"It was Stitch, chief; he was trying to rig a bomb or something," began Lucas.

Damon chambered another concussive round and casually pointed the weapon at Lucas's head.

"Try again," he said.

"The harvester has an orientation fault and I was trying to fix it," said Stitch, who had slowly risen to a seating position on the floor.

"He tried to call it in, but as usual Lucas 'forgot' to turn the transceiver on," said Giana, still wanting to put Lucas's Boltzmann through his head.

"He's getting unstable like the others," Lucas insisted, "They're not even human or machine and they are just looking for a chance to jump us."

"It doesn't help that you pull bits off them, beat them up or otherwise work them to death," Giana countered.

"Well we can just cut this one up and use his parts to stitch together on the next replacement Home Office sends," said Jack.

"There are no more left," said Damon. "They're saying all of the Breath-Takers near Mars were destroyed, and their parts too contaminated for us to use here."

Lucas opened his mouth to interrupt but Damon continued.

"What's more, Head Office on Earth have just informed me they have run out of Bion spares. This means Stitch is the last one we will ever see."

The chief then went on to complain about how the outer worlds always got the raw deal from the Inner Solar System. He ranted how they had to make do with using the former scourge of humanity to efficiently work their mining equipment and now that too had come to an end. But at least they hardly had to feed them and the things didn't need sleep.

They were right, Stitch thought. Having only a fraction of the organic material of an average human, Stitches' nutrient requirements were much less, thankfully making it almost impossible for his bosses to starve him to death. In fact, most of his energy needs were demanded by the mining and excavation tools he was forced to use, day after day.

"Now unless you want to take up the extra workload of operating the harvesters by yourself, I suggest you get back to your own job," Damon finished.

Stitch was back on the harvester, having recalibrated the part and getting outside as fast as he could. Not needing much protection, he had simply bounded out the airlock, whereas Lucas and other antagonists would need to 'dress up', giving Stitch time to get away.

The spark-sized sun set as Stitch's harvester conquered yet another farrow of rock-hard water-ice, leaving the landscape to be bathed in the eerie blue of nearby Neptune. These times he liked the most, his enhanced vision bringing the stars closer. Occasionally he would try to find distant Earth through the harvester's optical system. His home world. Memories of the Bio Wars came in fragments, but part of his 'rehabilitation' was to radically alter his long term memories. The miner's Semi-professional spare part dismemberment and reconstitution also didn't help his recall.

No, Stitch decided he didn't want to return to, or even go near the inner Solar System. Instead, he pointed the optics outward. He could just see the exhaust of the latest interstellar ship, bound for distant stars, and fuelled from his harvested volatiles. He wondered what it would be like, travelling to the stars.

A miniature explosion that severed his connection to the harvester broke his thoughts. His Bion instincts launched him out of the harvester and onto the hard ice, while his enhanced hearing heard the muffled noise of the shot that reached him through Triton's ultra-thin atmosphere.

The distant Lucas tried again with the other barrel, firing another shot at Stitch. As the hapless Bion again leapt out of the way, his automated target recognition system kicked in, triangulated Lucas's position, and attempted to command a weapon response. At this point Stitch's central nervous system locked up, as the 'weapon response' amounted to switching on the harvester lights, the Bion having long lost his weapons. Thankfully, while the Boltzmann was a feared weapon on Earth, it left a lot to be desired operating on the low gravity of Triton, especially in the hands of an amateur.

Whether it was the lights or something else, no more shots were fired. Stitch called in a harvester stoppage for the second time and cautiously made his way back to the base.

Even though he went through the opposite entrance from where the shots came from, Lucas was waiting for him.

Taking advantage of most of the miners supporting the Kuiper Belt run, Lucas subjected the bion to another savage beating.

"Perhaps I deserve this," thought the controller as distant memories of being connected to the War-net began to surface between blows. Fragmented images of targeting solutions on populated areas, human soldiers running for their lives, all flashed through Stitch's vision.

As he was cobbled together from several Bion subsystems, he could never be sure which of the memories were actually his or those from another individual. By the time of Foxhound most of the Bions were operating collectively anyway, sharing thoughts, tactics and planning through their war net.

"Stand by for Kuiper Belt Return!" an amplified voice interrupted the controller's thoughts and Lucas's beating.

Looking up weakly despite the damage he had sustained, Stitch saw the shift manager looking out of his viewing box. He was looking at Lucas in a death stare, and knew that announcing the Kuiper team arrival before their actual time would force him to stop torturing Stitch. Once again, the abused Bion slipped out from Lucas's reach to begin additional and hasty repairs. He last saw Lucas go up to the shift controller's room and his enhanced hearing meant he heard the ensuing conversation, even if he didn't want to.

"What did the chief just say about Stitch? I saw you take pot shots at the harvester too. You are out of control Lucas!"

"You saw nothing." Stitch could imagine the sneer on the larger man's face.

"I know that your sister died on Mars from the Breath-takers. My grandfather died in the Bio wars too; but…" the words were cut off and Stitch could imagine the noises he heard next were of Lucas throwing the shift manager on his back and his hands at his throat.

"I said you saw nothing." Lucas said to his now silent victim. "I don't care about your grandfather or you taking sides with the machines, while you hide in here spying on the rest of us working."

"You know there are thousands of ways to die out here," Lucas continued. "Accidental depressurisation of a dome compartment, your spacesuit waste heat activating a nitrogen smoker, or even just getting lost on the ice and running out of air."

Lucas continued with his captive audience, seeming to relish the thought of abandoning his victim in the wilderness at the edge of space. "No one would know where to start looking for you, and out here, no one would care. You saw nothing."

With the last remark Lucas bounded out of the room, leaving the shift manager muttering between gasps: "Be careful to check your space suit today".

The dangerous - and mostly unseen - work of mining the Kuiper Belt. Operators and their machines worked in permanent twilight.

Loping into the EVA suit room, Lucas suddenly came up against Damon, casually but firmly holding his concussive weapon.

"Just clearing something up with the shift manager, chief," Lucas said, trying to get past.

Damon's weapon didn't move. Lucas, realising his next move might be his last, prudently stayed where he was.

"Great," began Damon. "This means that for probably the first time, you will actually work hard and help the shift recover the Kuiper Belt team. If, before the end of the shift, you submit your application to transfer back to the inner Solar System, I would consider the matter totally cleared up."

Lucas had no choice but to accept Damon's help in getting suited up in the airlock.

"These suits are old," Damon said as he went through the check list of fixing, and activating various life support systems. "We're overdue for life support spares in these backpacks, so best stay close to the dome in case anything goes wrong."

A more subdued Lucas was glad to get outside following the chief's help, and gladder still once he performed a recheck of all his vital systems, just in case.

Despite the violence, the next Triton 'day', almost six Earth-days long, saw the mining team work as the productive unit it was meant to be. The Kuiper Belt Unit finished their aerobraking around Neptune. They sequestered part of their cargo of mined volatiles into on-orbit processing machines. These would fuel the next wave of interstellar-bound spacecraft. The balance of the harvest was deposited in the shallow gravity well of Triton for bulk processing.

Stitch was forever bound to Triton, his masters making modifications to prevent him leaving the moon, even to help the Kuiper Belt team. Instead, his "War-net" of connections between the various processer units allowed him to be at least virtually present. It also allowed him to see much more than most of the mining team. The space-suited shift manager working the ground team. Giana, with her powerful arms, swinging ice blocks into the processing train. Lucas, working on the thermal exchange systems, and also looking at Giana when he didn't think she was looking.

"Is that creep still watching?" a tele-message flashed up into Stitch's system from Giana.

"Yes, I'm afraid so," Stitch messaged back.

"At least Lucas can't hear us, the advantages of being part machine I guess," Giana virtually replied.

The tele-messaging existed outside the miner's communication system, and was essentially a machine-human interface Giana had developed from the old Bion systems.

A sudden spike in the system Lucas was monitoring threatened a thermal runaway. He had to shift his gaze from Giana and concentrate on what he was doing.

"Did you do that?" Giana virtually giggled.

"Possibly," Stitch sent back. "He looked like he needed some more work to do."

"Careful; he might find out, then that would really be the end," messaged Giana.

"Maybe that would be a good thing. I'm getting more memories from the war, I think. Now I am seeing people dying." Stitch sent, thinking back to the targeting memories he was experiencing more of lately.

"I am not surprised you are seeing things given how many times that creep has hit you since coming here. Anyway, they could just be something you remember from another Bion."

"Maybe, maybe not. I'm the last one now Giana. If not Lucas, then someone else will have their way, or I just break down permanently out here." If it was physically possible, Stitch would have shivered, thinking of himself, the last of his kind, unceremoniously disposed of in the Triton wastes.

"What do you really want, I mean really?" a virtually exasperated Giana messaged back.

Stitch sent through an image of the Milky Way, stars burning through his enhanced vision.

"I want to be free Giana. Take the sky, travel to the stars, like those interstellar ships we fuel."

"Well keep dreaming big guy, I think Damon is about to dump some more Kuiper blocks for us to process before end of shift." Giana clicked off the net.

Many hours later, shift change-over occurred, with a hustle-bustle of tired humans desperate to hand over to fresher-faced colleagues.

Stitch's attention was drawn to some talk outside the usual shift-change banter.

"Come on Lucas, don't hold the shift up."

A few moments silence, then: "Lucas, shut down the exchanger and come in, your consumables are low and you need to get back in."

More of the miners were shifting their attention to Lucas. Two were bounding to his position, still not moving from the thermal system.

"Lucas, what's wrong? You need to do an oxygen purge, right now!" Rhett demanded as he neared his colleague.

About this time Damon, had just come outside to try and help what was becoming an emergency, suddenly started to feel sick. He was halfway through a bounding arc – the equivalent of a run in Triton's low gravity, when he suddenly threw up.

Stitch saw Damon land awkwardly and collapse on the ice. He and three other miners rushed over to their boss, and struggled to get him up and back into the dome. As they made their way inside, they saw Lucas's suit suddenly stiffen upright as Rhett super-pressurised it with his auxiliary oxygen supply.

Damon, now unconscious, was rapidly unsuited and hooked up to ventilator equipment in the dome's makeshift medical area. A quick medical examination showed he had choked on his own vomit, and would need to be closely watched for at least the next Triton 'day'.

Lucas's frosted over helmet pulled off with a pop, a flurry of ice crystals invading the room as his overpressure spacesuit suddenly equalised. A second miner medic came close and saw that even without a medical examination it was clear that the miner was dead. Not only dead but stone cold.

"Lucas, LUCAS!" Rhett started screaming as several miners scrabbled at the dead man's suit to find out what went wrong.

The dome rapidly became a gaggle of semi-panicked, angry miners. It took a screaming match before the shift manager, frozen to the spot, finally agreed to call in a base distress.

The medics were the ones to finally regain some sort of control, and did their best to stabilise Damon and conduct an examination on Lucas. Despite several protests, a red-eyed Rhett would not move from his fallen friend.

"His coolant regulator gave out," someone said. Without it, the environmental control system in the backpack would have bathed Lucas's body in liquid chilled by Triton's cryogenic cold. Following a basic exam, the medic realised the chilling process was incredibly quick. Lucas would barely have had time to whimper before rapidly succumbing to extra-terrestrial hypothermia.

In the next room, the assistant medic had just finished with Damon and held up a finger covered in brownish ooze.

"Contaminated air supply," he said to the shift manager. "His breather hose was coated in this ooze. In a way he was lucky, getting sick like that. Must have been a reaction to the smell. Otherwise, he could have just fallen asleep in his suit, and no one would have noticed before it was too late."

"S-Someone deliberately did this to the chief?" the shift manager looked back, horrified.

A sudden commotion broke out in the main area, and the shift manager rushed out to see what was going on. Rhett, who had somehow got hold of Lucas's Boltzmann, was screaming at Stitch.

"You! You did this! You waited until we were all busy with the Kuiper harvest and turned off his cooler!"

"It could have been an accident, idiot. You know how old these suits are," cut in Giana.
The barrel swung to her chest. "Stay out of this Halfer! For all I know you could have planned this with the Breath-taker. Who of us was next? Tell me!"

"C-Calm down Rhett," the shift manager stammered. "We should get all the facts in first before jumping in too quickly to do things we might regret."

Rhett was having none of it. "Get back to your weakling boss, you snivelling ladder-climber. You know how this thing is linked to the mining equipment and harvester controls. How hard would it be to tap into Lucas' suit and turn his regulator off?"

Stitch could see the changes in body language of most of the other miners, as they slowly put two and two together. The Bion was indeed linked to most of the mine's systems. In fact, several in the room had a direct hand in making the links in the first place.

The shift manager, being surprisingly brave in his limited way, tried again. "This isn't helping, Rhett. Help is on the way, let's try to work through the facts together and help each other out."

While he said this, he had unclipped his version of Damon's concussive weapon and clumsily tried to fire it at Rhett. The other man more or less saw it coming and fired the Boltzmann, hurling the shift manager across the room.

The sound of the Boltzmann triggered a rush of images through Stitch's head. Soldiers battling Bions, nuclear flashes following Foxhound's strike. Humans and machines fighting, dying. He knew it was finally his turn to go.

Stitch, last of his kind, got up and rushed at Rhett, making sure he moved slowly enough for even a rank amateur to have time to aim and fire, ending it all.

***

"This operation certainly leaves a lot to be desired," the new mining chief said, his fresh face contrasting with the sorry countenances of the people before him.

"How much work do you expect to get done with just one arm?" he said to the female bionic missing most of her left appendage.

In response she, like the other miners, kept looking at the floor.

"And somehow one of the Kuiper harvesters has gone missing," he went on. With a final disgusted look at the staff before him, he turned away to let his second in command continue the briefing.

"Know now that this facility is under new management. What happened before has been dealt with and I expect not to hear of it again," stated the new man, clearly displaying his concussive weapon. "What I do expect is for everyone here to do their job, and follow the rules. If that is too much, then there is the exit, and trust me, it is a *very* long walk home."

In almost no time the newly-arrived relief crew, easily outnumbering the existing miners, made themselves at home on the base and let everyone know in no uncertain terms that they were in charge.

***

The azure blue of Neptune was now just a pinpoint of light among the stars. The sun glinted off the shiny left arm of the Kuiper harvester's sole occupant. Stitch's thoughts were finally quiet, finally out of range of the Triton net. The net had saved his life, though, his personality being reconstituted from portions scattered amongst the harvesters and machinery when Rhett had shot out the original. He also had Lucas's murderer to thank for being out here.

"Stitch! Get up, time to go!" Giana had said.

"Go where?" he had replied stupidly as he slowly realised he was alive. Giana had stolen time and cobbled together parts between shifts to rebuild the Bion's body. Stitch wasn't through asking silly questions though: "Why did you do it?"

"Lucas would have killed you. He nearly did it to Damon. And it was easy to use our net to hack that creep's suit. In a way, he also gave us a break."

"How?" Stitch thought. Giana pulled him up in the light Triton gravity, and he saw for the first time a Kuiper harvester, waiting quietly on the ice.

"I can't give you the stars, but I can get you the next best thing".

"Why don't you come with me," Stitch offered. "Half a person plus part of a person…"

"Almost makes a whole person," Giana finished for him, grinning.

"You know I can't, not enough food for two. Anyway, in a very real sense, part of me is going with you."

Stitched noticed, for the first time, that Giana was minus her left arm. He looked where it was in its new home at the end of his shoulder.

Not quite the stars, but close, the last Bion squinted as a bright flash briefly filled the harvester's cockpit. An interstellar ship, had just sent its cargo of brave explorers out of the Solar System. Starry-eyed hopefuls who would never know what it cost to fill their spacecraft's propellant tanks.

(Above) Advances in propulsion reduced dependance on the the Kuiper Belt mining monopoly. Supporters wave on an interstellar mission launched closer to the Sun and receiving a gravity boost from Uranus.

THE WINGS OF LEGEND

(Above) Deep oceanographic surveys discovered ruins whose purpose initially puzzled their discoverers. It was some time before they became associated with the Narriwa legend.

A bulbous cylinder drifted through the voids of the Milky Way. This probe had been travelling for eight years - all alone once it had left the mother craft whose feeble signals had to travel for millions of kilometres before reaching its lonely child.

Over long years, the probe's battery of sensors tirelessly scanned the cosmos for any evidence that would prove the presence of an alien life form. Along with 80 of its sisters, the probe had been sent on this mission purely because of a distant legend.

Endlessly surveying cold space and nothing more, the legend seemed to be nothing more than a child's tale. Suddenly the probe's radiometers registered a strong signal, different from the random crackle and hiss of interstellar space. Autonomous command systems traced the signal to its source, a wan star in the distance. The craft's long-dormant propulsion system erupted to life, and set the craft on a course that would change history.

As the probe approached the star; its sensors began to pick up other signals. It registered short

The historic encounter between the Irs probe and a Terran exploratory mission led to the meeting of Captain Coleman Breen with the Irs leader. This caused the formation of the Galactic Alliance a few months later. On that date, entire worlds celebrated as both Earth and Irs finally found their lost counterpart after centuries of separation.

"In the name of humanity of the planet Irs, I welcome you and offer you wishes of peace and good will."

"On behalf of my people of Earth, I thank you for your kindness and also send you hope of a prosperous future for both our worlds."

"These two phrases have since became famous as they mark the first physical encounter man has made with an extra-terrestrial race," said host Judy Gilligan, presenting literally a galactic broadcast.

"These exchanges also led to the joining of our two cultures," she continued. "Members of each race saw their alien counterparts as beings that were almost identical to themselves."

In stark contrast to Judy's lofty introduction, the backgrounds and individual characteristics of the four people sitting with her could not have been more different. In fact, the only similarity they shared was being in the same room and contributing to the first official verbal contact.

Marshal Coleman Breen, formerly Captain Breen, sat on the left of the program host and was the first to shake hands with an alien. The alien he shook hands with was the Irs' president, the leader, Karn Slikchovix. This unforgettable day would define their identities for the rest of their lives.

Yet, these two men were not the ones that drew Judy Gilligan's attention. Instead, her inquisitive mind was drawn to Jason Merandez, the former Craft Commander of the REA-1d3 mission undertaken by the Remote Exploratory Association. A woman that was considerably younger than the other guests, Sile Dogannis, daughter of the late Heros Dogannis who founded the Irs mission to launch probes into the Milky Way, also engaged Judy Gilligan's attention.

"Thank you to you both for joining us," Judy's high-pitched voice added after greeting the president and Captain Breen. Her voice rang out through the studio as she adjusted her microphone: "Now, before we before we begin, I think it is best if we review the transcript that Jason has with him describing the mission that accidently made contact with the Irs probe."

Jason smiled in return, "Thanks Judy. This transcript in my hand holds the actual transmissions that occurred between the mother craft, Control and the EVA team commencing about two minutes before the discovery. At that time, the first successful planet fall had been undertaken and the EVA team were travelling to their first ground coordinate via a surface rover."

The video in the centre of the room sprung to life and the transcript commenced.

EVA: We are at coordinates 24.33N, 72.74W of TDS <touch down site>.

COM: Copy, proceed on course for first waypoint.

EVA: Affirm. We have a visual on waypoint.

COM: Prepare for egress and package deployment... <at this point a piercing series of whistles and clicks caused by a yet undetected alien probe breaks through transmission>.

EVA: Say again Com, you're fading.

COM: Roger fading. We're checking diagnostics. What is your current status?

EVA: We are waypoint one... <shrill noise breaks in again>.

COM: We've lost your last. We suspect that your primary transmitter is unserviceable. Prepare to

Out of fuel, one of many interstellar probes launched by Irs, drifts near a Mars-like planet. Its mission to seek the source of the Narriwa legend was unsuccessful.

use backup frequencies.

EVA: Affirm, give us the word.

PROBE: Proceed on course to first waypoint.

EVA: Say again, Com?

COM: That last transmission didn't come from us <at this moment a proximity warning alerts Mission Control of an incoming object>.

EVA: We have a proximity alert. Stand by while we assess it.

COM: Affirm. Standing by.

<Voice transmissions cease for a few moments while Control deals with the proximity alert. Then…>…

EVA: Com we are Green Angel. Repeat, we are Green Angel!

COM: Say again? Please confirm status.

EVA: We are confirmed Green Angel. Contingency procedures are now in effect!

"Please tell us what were those strange noises we heard, like whistles and the repetitions of some of the transmissions." Judy turned back to Sile Dogannis after the video fell silent.

"The probe was originally designed to send a coded message of greetings across a wide range of frequencies. This was so that any race would be able to receive and interpret it. At the same time, the probe relayed the news of contact back to Irs."

"What about the repetition of REA-1d3's transmissions?" she asked.

Sile explained further, "When the probe alerted Irs, it was quite close to the Terran spacecraft and was clearly receiving the transmissions between it and the lander's crew. Of course, the Terran language couldn't be understood, so the scientists on Irs thought it would be a good idea to use their own language."

As was obvious by the video, the REA crew couldn't understand the language and they simply mistook it for transmission faults. However, when they ran diagnostics no issues arose and by then they had heard the proximity alert. Shortly afterwards, the REA crew discovered the Irs probe firsthand.

Judy continued with her questions. "Now Jason, I wonder if you could explain a few things further. For example, what does the term Green Angel mean?"

"Green Angel was the code name for any extra-terrestrial craft or being we encountered. We used it because originally, people of Earth associated aliens with little green men. As for Angels, they are of course beings that can fly. Since the code name was used for alien flying objects, we thought it was appropriate."

"When did you first know you weren't alone up there?" Judy asked, her body language indicating her great intrigue.

"Proximity warnings are usually used to alert us of any incoming meteors or other things similar to that, which come too close to our spacecraft. At first, we thought that was what it was. But when our telescopes started taking pictures, we noticed that the 'meteor' was following a smooth trajectory and finally realised that it was in fact an alien."

"What does 'contingency procedures' mean and what did you do when this was called?"

Jason stiffened slightly at the question: "In the occurrence of a Green Angel, all communications will cease and all mission data will be deleted. Afterwards, the EVA team also had to abort their mission and return to their lander in preparation for emergency take-off. The aim of this procedure was to ensure that the astronauts would return safely back on Earth in the event that this unknown probe turned out to be hostile."

Judy gasped loudly and seemed genuinely offended and skeptical at the thought of the Irs people meant any ill will to the Earthlings. Jason knew that she thought the notion was absurd, but then she wasn't as young as the Commander and she didn't know much about his feelings towards aliens. Judy wouldn't have been surprised if his views hadn't been influenced by modern films or human intents to future segregate from possible alien societies.

He also remembered how on edge the crew was at the news of a new inhabited planet and how they all shared the mixed emotions of excitement, wonder, fear and confusion. Once Jason had given instructions to risk an encrypted message back to Earth explaining the encounter – this had sparked a chain reaction in the arrival of a Terran craft full of academics, all hoping to take a glimpse of the craft and pick up any information possible. A few military cruises were also put on standby in case things turned sour.

After the arrival of these academics, in exchange, a larger alien craft approached the Earth to investigate the humans. It projected what looked like a video showing images of an alien world featuring blue oceans and a wonderful landscape. Then a human face appeared and began to talk in a foreign language.

Jason continued his recount to Judy, "At that point, we all breathed a collective sigh of relief. At least they weren't some red-eyed monsters and neither were we. But, at the same time, we were all amazed and mystified. I mean: real people living on another world!"

Judy smiled and returned to Sile, "Now, are we able to hear Irs's point of view on the contact? I understand that Irs has adopted a similar cautious standpoint to the Green Angle scenario?"

"Yes. Our folklore had always described the Terran planet, the Earth as a warmongering race and even after thousands of years, the mission designers were still very anxious about a possible hostility. The legend of Narriwa, which my father had deciphered years ago, was taken very seriously. Nevertheless, our probe didn't detect any type of weaponry on the Earth craft, so it initiated first contact."

Judy frowned, "Myself and, I'm sure, the audience too, we are confused about what the Narriwa legend is. Could you please explain its story to us and its relevance to the Irs probes?"

Sile began her recount: "The Narriwa legend captured Heros' attention decades before the creation of the Wayward Project. Prior to working with probes, Heros was a terrestrial historian. His dream was not only to understand what it was asking, but to also fulfil it.

"Everyone called him a lunatic," she continued, "chasing after loose threads that had been destroyed long ago. Yet, he persuaded some sponsors that he had pieced together scraps of information taken from our folklore about another civilisation and then he presented it to Sile in the clearest form. The Narriwa legend was finally brought to light once more. The legend outlines a mass exodus of people from a distant star who eventually settle on a desolate world – a planet that Heros determined to be Irs. However, these pioneers where unsatisfied by their dead, empty surroundings, so they used magic called 'Narriwa' to paint the ground in various shades of greens and blues. Now, the land was gorgeous, and Mother Nature began to do her work and bloom more flowers and singing birds that flew high up into the skies. Another neighbouring planet was also inhabited: it was known as Mortem, but the magic of Narriwa was not needed as it was already beautiful. Despite this, Irs was by far the most breathtaking land as it prospered due to climate change, and as a result, the people of Mortem became jealous of Irs pioneers for they lacked contentment and good fortune. Soon a war broke out between these two planets, which lasted for decades. This conflict caused so much suffering for thousands of people. Many innocent lives were lost, simply out of jealousy. The legend also chronicled a tragic end: Mortem destroyed, its beauty lost to seas of fire, and Irs almost sharing a similar fate if not for their final attack. The legend states that the fighters within Irs threw a heavy mountain onto the far off enemy and this broke their spirits.

"After this calamity, all acts of war had ceased and Irs began its restoration to former glory. Mortem was forgotten in time as men and women walked freely among Irs. If not for Heros' work, the legend might have not come to light for centuries.

"Fortunately, Heros lived within the age of modern technology when people were open to new ideas, so the legend of Narriwa was finally taken seriously.

"Although it explained how the people of Irs came to the planet, there were still numerous questions within the legend that captured the curiosity of many. For example, was the planet Mortem a hot and barren world that orbited close to its sun or the victim of an artificial, human made disaster? Heros believed that the cause of its destruction was a nuclear attack due to two things: the fused and cratered surface and the planet's radioactive atmosphere.

"However, over time the Narriwa legend was proven wrong as there was no further evidence to support it and Heros's theory was discredited until a deep ocean survey made a discovery ten years later. As if by fate, a remote oceanic mapper was scouting the ocean floor when it came across what was thought as an ancient shipwreck resting in a crater.

"Yet, as cameras zoomed in, it appeared as though the seaweeds had hidden a structure that had no resemblance to anything that had previously floated on Irs's seas.

"The decaying structure was beginning to crumble under its own weight. Explorers had to investigate the insides of the construction quickly and effectively before it was lost forever. The inside revealed numerous floor boards which contained the corroding remains of unidentifiable equipment. Architects determined the unknown vessel to be a spacecraft due to its sturdy hull and artificially in-built gravity appearance. This was not the only piece of information that baffled scientists, but also the engraving along the ship's side. Ancient inscriptions were deciphered to be Nar Sel Aviaa, equivalent to Unit 9, in the Irs tongue.

"Heros put forward the idea that this is where the word Narriwa derived from. If so, this would mean that the legend bore truth and Irs was in fact a colonist planet. Its inhabitants were their descendants who terraformed Irs through magic or, according to more probable explanation, by the usage of on incredibly advanced climate change technology.

"After this discovery, Heros founded the Wayward Project and soon the Andromeda Galaxy began to be explored. Unmanned warp probes were designed to rapidly cross the gulfs of empty space and detect the presence of any life form.

"This is when Heros' theories were put forward and tested by the public. Their response was more answers to questions and not just a simple child's fairy tale. However, Heros used this as an opportunity to explore both the Milky Way Galaxy and the rest of Andromeda. Finally, after two long years, a new fleet of probes was created and this time they were designed to cross the two million light year distance – and not a small distance within his solar system.

"Sadly, Heros did not live to see the day when all his hard work made possible the first contact. He never saw the fruits of his work fulfilled."

After Sile told her story, Judy paused for a moment and then started on a new track. "Thank you Sile. Now that the Wayward project has been covered, I would like us to move onto the next major event, the historic flight taken by Captain Coleman Breen to Irs. Marshal Breen, could you please tell us what the flight was like and what happened during it?"

One of the most famous men alive, Marshal Breen took the floor, "Thank Judy for bringing me here.

(Above) First Contact. At the limits of its endurance, an Irs probe encounters an Earth mission exploring an extra-solar planetary system.

What an honour it is to be able to be able to participate in the anniversary of the Galactic Alliance. After we had exchanged as much information with the craft as we could, we decided it was time to meet the race we had been searching for. So, after much planning and thought, we considered that a flight to Irs would be the best way to respond to their first contact, ensuring that our planets would create an agreement of some sort of peaceful cooperation and so forth."

"You make the mission sound so simple!" Judy laughed softly.

"It was anything but simple. We travelled a thousand times further than ever before and it took us 10 long years to reach uncharted territories, which lie many light years away from Earth. If anything had gone wrong, we would have been essentially stranded. Thank goodness, nothing major occurred and the people of Irs were kind and gave us a warm greeting." Marshal Breen paused, as if imagining what might have happened if things didn't go smoothly aboard his flight.

"There were twenty personnel aboard our craft, some of which were representatives from the seven major governments as well as some distinguished members of academic backgrounds."

As Marshal Breen continued outlining the details of his mission, his mind wandered into the past, the morning when he piloted through the Irs's atmosphere with the Unified Earth and REA flags.

The sun on Irs dawned, and slowly the contents of the meeting place were revealed. Nineteen faces were glued to the craft's windows as the Irs landscape flew past. Then the passenger of the Terran craft saw a large city dominated by the largest stadium ever created by man, at which they gazed in wonder, trying to grasp its full size as they were preparing to land.

As Breen and the escort banked over the landing point, they noticed thirty million people sitting within the stadium. All were eagerly awaiting his arrival. The rising of their sun was used as a symbol of the awaking of a new age when all their questions would be answered, and new ones would arise for the benefit of both civilisations.

While the first ever Terran spaceship landed on the platform safely, Breen's nerves began to creep up and, explicably, he tried to delay the first meeting by double checking all his landing checks. The moment finally arrived.

As the airlock opened with a hiss and the lander's exit point was flooded with the glare from the alien sun, the passengers' ears were deafened by the cheers of thirty million people. Breen's mind went blank, and even years later he could not recount to Judy the unreal feeling of stepping out of the craft and breathing in fresh alien air. Nor did he remember saying the famous greeting to Karn Slikchovix, the famous representative of the Irs Council.

Sitting beside Breen in the interview room, Karn Slikchovix adopted the same look as he returned to the moment when the Terran craft reached his stadium. Once Breen's craft had passed into the Irs stratosphere, Karn had ensured that they would be greeted by no less than two hundred Irs spacecrafts. He remembered standing on the platform as Breen landed, and realising that Heros's dream regarding the Narriwa legend were at last fulfilled.

His mind also raced with questions about planet Earth. Was their sun the same colour as the sun that bathed him with her glorious light every time he woke up in the morning?

Did their ocean waves sound like music as they crashed onto the shore? What drinks and food did they consume, and would they be able to provide them to Irs?

Later, when the humans approached Karn and shook his hand, two famous greetings were said and then strongly debated ever since. They were carefully recorded and broadcast to the people of both worlds, and represented an era of peace to be remembered for as long as their nations existed.

This exchange of words had sparked celebrations and cheers among the crowds of all known inhabited worlds.

The televised interview drew to a close as billions of people turned away from their screens to celebrate the anniversary of the first contact. As a final tribute to the heroic efforts of the people behind this project - and especially to Heros, the dreamer - this speech was broadcast during the two congressional meetings held on Irs and Earth, and then circulated on each media channel and social platform: "To all the colonies and people of humanity: I, Marshal Breen, representative of our cultures, am happy to bring you this message of hope. Today marks a turning point in the history of humankind. We have discovered a race of people separated from us by millions of light years in space-time and thousands of years in time. They are our new friends in our time of need; they are our new allies to help us end this war with Mars. Today marks the formation of the Inter Galactic Alliance - in which we venture together into the future, with a mutual spirit of peace and discovery."

(Above) Concerted engineering and planning efforts spanned two civilisations to culminate in an Earth mission physically visiting the Irs homeworld. The Terran delegation was met with unprecedented celebrations as they were escorted to their landing site.

FROM RED TO GREEN

(Above) The Phobos Station had been established in orbit near Mars' largest Moon for decades. Originally a staging post for surface missions, it became a key way-station for the Mars terraforming process.

For many scholars, Mars was the true starting point for First Contact, and the creation of the Alliance. It was on this barren, red planet that the first signs of another human race were discovered. Decades of scouring the red deserts revealed a diversity of ruins and artifacts of great interest to human geographers and archaeologists. For all the exploration, though, the pyramids of Mars were still shrouded in mystery. Extensive research revealed nothing else apart from what has already been concluded. Since their discovery, thousands of tons of regolith were excavated to reveal doors at the bases of each pyramid. Many tools and techniques had been used to try to open them, all resulting in complete failure. There was brief talk of using tactical nuclear devices to melt through. Fortunately these plans were hastily taken off the table, never mentioned again.

The other artifacts found in sandy or rocky environments all contributed to the creation of a fairly accurate reconstruction of Mars's prehistoric ecosystem. Ancestors of the pyramid makers had somehow transformed a cold, icy world into one that could support life. Could the Red Planet be coaxed back to its former green glory? The Alliance Council debated the issue extensively before early plans to terraform Mars were set in action.

The ensuing years saw the ice moons of Jupiter and millions of tons of comet material being mined for their precious water ice. Mass drivers were set to collect this precious element, and companies were formed to send it streaming down into the Martian atmosphere. This process continuously added to the scant water supplies of this half-Earth-sized planet.

At the same time, masses of aerial fusion explosions were set off, which vaporised the once frozen gases at Mars's poles and subterranean Martian resources. This process was assisted by specially-engineered bacteria that explosively spread over the Martian desert, breaking down the soil to release great amounts of oxygen trapped inside the underground minerals.

The watering of Mars and the thickening air began to feed on itself, and unimaginable events of progress quickly became apparent. Decades after the first comets impacted Mars, alien rains began to fall. Life was starting to flourish on most regions of the planet.

Only ten years after the first recorded rains, astronaut Ronnie Bloom strode purposely from his domed habitat Taking onlookers by surprise, he took off his space suit's helmet and breathed Martin air. Unlike the first tentative attempts, Bloom was able to sustain his body's oxygen levels indefinitely. Others followed Bloom outside, marveling at their new freedom. Further advances were made until Mars was officially declared green again and a habitable place without artificial protection from the Alliance.

The Martian pyramids rested unchanged, as they had done for millennia, throughout the terraforming process. Investigations into the Martian ruins were well advanced; similar efforts against the pyramids remained stalled for lack of new findings. They stood tall above the new Martian grass and cast huge shadows on research teams assembled outside each of their entrances. These doors had never opened since they were last closed by the race who built them.

Team leader Laura, standing in the pyramid shadows, admonished her crew members one last time. "We are all here because environmental sensors have detected a change in the pyramids' spectrum. We don't yet know what this means, but make sure your environment suit is active and perform a buddy check." Laura and a fellow researcher performed one last suit cross check. Then, absently nearing one of the pyramids sealed doors, nearly fell over when, without warning, the entrance suddenly opened. Almost immediately all doors leading to the remaining pyramids opened, causing an explosion of wild chatter on the researchers' communication channel. Whether this was a coincidence or the doors were programmed to open on this date was unknown.

The eventual completion of the terraforming process marked the restoration of Mars as a contemporary nexus for humanity.

Laura and other team leaders had their work cut out for them trying to restore a semblance of order to the group. Some over-hasty volunteers wishing to gain early access to the pyramids were stopped in no uncertain terms. Laura's direction was clear. No person was to set foot over the pyramid threshold until a thorough robotic safety inspection had been completed.

Michael, Laura's safety officer, carefully monitored the data returning from the robot scouts. "So far so good," he said in answer to Laura's question. "The environment inside this pyramid seems as good as what we are experiencing on the outside. Of course, there is only one way to really find out."

It took another two days after the doors were opened before Laura and her team was allowed to physically enter the first pyramid. When Michael stepped through, he noticed that they were moving into a dark corridor. The air inside was safe; they did not have to worry about any rare, dangerous gases - only a musty smell. However, they all kept the environmental suits tucked close to their skin.

Outside, they had left all the equipment used to try and open the doors since they didn't need it any longer. Instead, they all used communication and navigation devices along with other special equipment to help them find their way inside the pyramidal labyrinth.

The team had been split into smaller groups so they could cover more area of the pyramid they were assigned to. Michael and a few others had taken the left turn from the main corridor. They had only been exploring for a few minutes when the lack of familiarity caused Michael to lose his sense of time, which for him seemed to have stopped completely. Only when his communicator system blinked did Michael realise that five minutes had passed since his last radio call. He was meant to provide his location and status every five minutes. All team member's bodily functions and movements were monitored anyway, but Michael felt as though it was important to add a personal touch to the official recording, even if the mission control staff back outside the pyramids didn't seem to need that sort of reassurance.

"Adams, Team 3, still within left wing hallway. Nothing to report," Michael spoke with a subdued tone into his microphone. It seemed strange to talk any louder - already the harsh echoes of his team's movements and the bright torchlight cutting through the dust seemed intrusion enough on this ancient structure. Part of Michael was also worried that they might have awoken an old ghost, but it seemed foolish to him that anything could have survived for thousands of years without food, water, and sunlight.

After his radio call, Michael's team continued to venture through the hallway, taking detailed measurements of the Pyramid's interior. Despite their efforts, nothing new and interesting greeted them apart from bare stone floors and walls of similar construction to the well-studied pyramid exterior. Michael began to wonder how Laura's team was going in the adjacent pyramid when once more, his communicator blinked.

He halted his team and answered: "Adams, Team 3, nothing to repo-" Michael was cut off by a loud crash of equipment and series of clicks. He whirled around to see the rest of his crew run to the source of the commotion. At the centre was one of his team members stumbling after dropping some expensive equipment. Although Michael was furious with his clumsy teammate, he was more intrigued by what was behind him. What looked like just another part of the wall door began to slide open, as if by magic, to reveal a darkened room beyond.

Michael hastily reported the event to command and prepared to move his men inside the room. Four torchlights scanned the room, slowly revealing its contents. The beams occasionally hit a shiny surface, sending myriads of reflections skittering through the space. It was becoming apparent that whatever the pyramids had been hiding resided within this room.

As soon as the first human stepped into the room, overhead lights turned on. Rows of oblong shapes came into focus as the room brightened. They seemed to be a dull green colour and roughly the same length as a human body.

One of the men under his command made a joke about how it looked like a crypt. But as they approached, Michael realised that it was exactly what the team were seeing. Each of the objects was in fact a casket, and as he shone his torch beam through its translucent top, a dark, strangely familiar form seemed to stare back at him. Startled, Michael stumbled back and soon, the rest of the team froze in fright as well, as they saw for themselves what filled each casket. The room was filled with rows of dead bodies lying in state. Hollow eye sockets stared vacantly out of the caskets at the stunned team. Michael chanced another look and saw that intra-vehicular activity body suits of some form clung tight to each body. Other items, some looking vaguely similar to cooling garments and others whose function could only be guessed at, caught Michael's eye.

The investigator within him slowly regained control as the shock of the discovery wore off. Closer examination by the team showed that the caskets were not intended to be the final resting place for these carefully displayed bodies. The clothes and equipment all spoke of protection from the elements and the need for life support. Subsequent forensic analysis identified mechanisms meant to sustain the occupants through the passage of time; unconscious, but alive. However, for some unknown reason they died without ever waking up.

The furor rising from the discoveries within the pyramids were not lost on the respective Irs, Terran and burgeoning Martian governments. Laura was directed to mount a joint effort to investigate the pyramids thoroughly. Partway through planning the effort, Laura received an unwelcome interruption.

"Freya, I really don't have time for this. I have three governments pressing me to get an interstellar team working together on the pyramid caskets."

"I appreciate that, but..."

"Plus much of the rest of the universe is asking me if we should even be disturbing a sacred site, and you think I have time to listen to your historic analysis that doesn't even touch on the nature of the pyramids' caskets?"

Freya stood her ground. "I know our team focused on analyzing historic records found in the pyramids, not the bodies themselves, but we now know why they are there and what the pyramids are for."

Sensing something important, the overworked team lead paused. "Go on," she said.

Freya continued. "Our findings are quite clear. The society that built the pyramids was related to that of the Irs Narriwa legend. These pyramids were built to protect early Mars inhabitants from a war of some kind. We also think this war was the same one mentioned in the Narriwa legend, and was big enough to devastate pre-historic Mars as well."

To Laura, Freya's analysis started to make sense. An exodus, maybe from Earth's solar system, had somehow led to the terraforming of distant Irs and the destruction of another planet. Effects of the destruction had also been large enough to wipe out entire civilizations. Only ambiguous legends, shattered ruins and now Martian bodies were left behind for future generations to decipher.

"I wonder what it would have been like, living through that period of the Exodus?" Laura said, as much to herself as her colleague. She had little time for further thought. Yet another planning emergency cropped up; the Exodus problem temporarily forgotten.

THE EXODUS

(Above) Green Area 1, showing part of the critical infrastructure required to maintain an Earth-like environment for generations of explorers. Designated as one of two recreational zones, time allotted for visits to Green Area 1 was tightly monitored and enforced.

"Laura, I think we are onto something big here,' a frustrated Freya said to her boss. "Our research is on the verge of mapping out the pre-history of three major planetary systems but you keep cutting us back."

Laura, distracted as ever, had little time for yet another problem. "I have told you clearly that our directed priority is the analysis and preservation of the Martian pyramid bodies. Everything else is secondary to that."

Sensing the look on Freya's face, Laura hastily interjected, "However I have also been directed to work a joint team of Mars, Terran and Irs experts. I can spare you some limited resources from these."

Freya was ecstatic. Her skills at using limited resources rivaled that of her supervisor. Her interstellar group of experts pored over historic records and artifacts from exploratory missions across the cosmos, and compiled the most complete account of the Exodus to date. A summary of her work is displayed at the Galactic Museum of History: "Millennia ago, people watched as rockets launched into the air until all they could see was a tiny speck riding upon a million flames. Brave heroes were sent into the unknown universe where almost anything could go wrong. Despite this large, possible risk, humanity's curiosity pushed them to explore an ever receding frontier. Within a ridiculously short amount of time, millions of people had reached out and touched the stars that had, once upon a time, seemed impossible to reach. Thousands of star systems were catalogued, planets explored and moons settled.

The great distances measured in light years between the mother planets and their far distant colonies raised governance issues. Over time, the old Earth colonies made their own laws and slowly turned away from what was seen as a tyrannical Earthly kingdom. Earth's strict territorial claims on colonies and their associated draconian laws were falling out of favour to far distant governments.

The fragile days of peace came to an end. Quarrels over ownership and settlement rights became frequent among planets. As a result, many people left these settlements, as they once left Earth, in search for new homes, for peace and prosperity, hence venturing further into outer space than ever before.

Meanwhile, Earth ships straying into colony-controlled regions were increasingly finding themselves challenged, escorted from their territory or even fired upon. Eventually Earth's ruling council decided that the whole sorry affair had gone on long enough. Patronising speeches were broadcast to extol the virtues of a home-dominated government. They described how the Colonists' power was too fragmented to provide true interstellar stability. The colonists retaliated and suggested that they should gain their free right to govern through a just ruling which didn't violate Earth independence.

The speech war fuelled growing anger and dissension, polarising opinion between the home Solar System and the outlying colonies. Proximal conflicts broke out, with affected groups leaking out heart rending images of children and families killed in the attacks. Many on Earth sided with the colonist cause, and the chaos almost descended into a civil war. However, the response from the central government was swift; its vastly superior firepower ended the matter in a period of months. The members of the rebellion were arrested and were given a choice. They could either be executed on the spot, or they could spend the rest of their lives travelling in generational starships to a new destination. Thousands of people found themselves put into space aboard experimental spacecraft, in an event known as 'the Exodus'."

Freya's thorough work was also able to reconstruct life on board one of these Exodus ships...

Jack ran swiftly across the grass, artificial mist clinging to his legs. Despite the occasional tree rustling, His plundering footsteps were the only thing that was heard. But to his sensitive ears there was another smooth sound: that of the echoes betraying the fact that the ground beneath him was only few centimetres in depth.

To the people that were born aboard this ship, this fact was not evident. Nevertheless, the older man knew better; there was great difference between a solid Terran soil and the floor beneath him. Like all the original people to board the Exodus, the child inside him missed the crunching of real soil.

The mist that filled the large, green room brought back memories of past, free days. It also hid the framework ceiling high above which was the vaporous protection from reality. However, this was wearing thin for Jack as he knew from the forecast that the mist would only stay for another eleven minutes before a gentle breeze tore it to shreds. For now, he enjoyed the sight of fake grass, fake tress and the simulation of rolling hills in the distance. His clever trained eyes could even pick up the computerised trace of his destination, an artificial hill: Mount Pheasant.

Rising 200 metres from the ground, the highest 'mountain' in the 'green area' afforded the nicest view of this little land. Access to the top of this large and rare beauty was only granted for the very select few. Jack knew from bitter experience that many people who had experienced this freedom from the top of Mt Pheasant had never returned, as if this joy was a recompense for some sacrifice or work done onto their spacecraft.

Jack had met nearly all of these Exodus people in his role of one of the hundreds of councilors whose only function was to provide a human interface between broken people and the Enforcement. Broken people were people who had been torn from their spouses back on Earth and had to spend the rest of their lives here, nearly all alone. The Enforcement was the law that from time to time required people to 'volunteer' to be put to 'sleep' so the ship could save on oxygen and food supplies.

As his feet led him on, Jack's mind wandered elsewhere, to the past where a sad chain of events had brought him to share 40 square kilometres of vegetation and millions of tons of metal with ten thousand souls. That chapter of history for him was closed, but of course it would never be forgotten; it happened merely a decade ago when he was a teenager with the ability to remember well. The childish memories dwelled well inside him and during his darkest moments they emerged, as sad stories always do.

One of the clearest memories Jack had while aboard the Exodus was the Departure Day. The fleet of ships leaving their home were similar to the each other: all packed close together and housing at that time thousands of lonely, shattered souls. Then, in time, the fleet broke apart, each taken on different destinations, around various suns. Some saw this as a sign that they needed to be alone from others in order to form own civilisations, while others considered it a tragedy since unified, they had much more chances of survival.

As their home worlds disappeared – becoming a mere speck of colour and light, a wave of terror and sadness swept over Jack's shipmates. While most people began to break down sobbing and screaming, others withdrew and silently watched through the windows the empty space as if they were trying to keep Earth's presence in view forever. Jack remembered how he knew that only then his true work has about to begin and how excited he was. He left the window and made his way into the distressed crowd. In contrast to nearly everyone else who was forced onto this long and lonely journey, Jack had actually volunteered to be among them. The sense and thrill of an adventure had always appealed to him, so he was ready as all great councilors. There were very few of his kind as no government allowed much training or preparation for the Exodus.

Even though it was his job to help others through their troubles, Jack waited for people to process their worries and sad thoughts. He also wondered when they would set foot on real soil again, but unlike most, he still held firm to the hope of finding a habitable planet.

He told himself that he would explore all options as they came and encouraged many not to give up. He used prophetic, bright words to excite even the most pessimistic riders, and shared his plans in going further towards a new a life on unexplored lands.

In a few months, he found that with no Milky Way in sight, people actually enjoyed their confined spaces more than the open air and they didn't seem keen in landing on real ground soon.

In fact, after just one year people stopped even visiting the 'green areas'…despite the fact that the average citizen was required to spend a minimum of twenty hours a week in this healthy mental zone. This was recommended for them to relax from the week's duties and enjoy the nature that engineers had replicated based off Earth's beauty.

The green area had twin banks of bright, yellow light standing in to symbolise the sun at sunrise and sunset. Additionally, the landscape took on various hues that weren't too far off the terrestrial mornings. In the afternoon, the second bank took over, changing the bright 'green area' into a mix of light and shadows to depict the incoming sunset. There were also two artificial rivers, one lake and even constant rainfall for people to experience. Sadly, this small area would never fulfil older generation's dream of basking in real sunlight or tasting and smelling fresh rainfall.

A slight rumble brought Jack back into the present time. As he was jogging, he looked upwards and saw two airplanes breaking through the thin fog and racing low over the landscape, only to disappear once more through the mist. Very few vehicles were allowed in the 'Green area' and only for emergency reasons. However, these planes might have been normal since they provided a quick means of travel from this 'green area' to the next and no doubt they were part of the connecting tunnel heading for the new 'Green area 2' currently under construction, Jack thought.

The mist began to clear, allowing Jack to see clearly where he was heading. His route to Mt Pheasant deliberately took him past the main features of 'Green area 1'. His reflection gleamed in the water as he passed Lake Kannalis, a fresh body of water that offered a cool alternative to the summer months. In winter, the lake also served as an ice-skating rink as it became a huge freezer.

As he continued along the water's edge, he heard raised voices that caused him to run faster toward the source of the commotion. A man stood between his wife, a child and a squat mobile machine that had disrupted them from their morning swim. The Enforcement.

"Just a little bit longer, please," the man was saying with a shaky voice. "It's my son's fifth birthday and I'm teaching him how to swim. The shift was really hard this time around."

A clear and forceful voice cut him off: "Your allocated time in the green area has expired. Please vacate the area immediately and make your way to Exit Four."

"You don't understand - please, only a few more minutes!" the man frantically tried to convince the officer while holding his hands together as in a fervent prayer.

"The rules of occupancy are quite clear; I insist, you MUST vacate the area now and in an orderly fashion," an uncooperative enforcer stated.

Jack knew the rules of occupancy, as everyone on board did. While in the 'Green area', everyone's time, including Jack's, were closely monitored by the Enforcement. So, at the end of their allocated time, they were to leave and return to work, in order to enable to next shift of workers to enjoy their free time.

It quickly became clear to Jack that the man wasn't backing down, neither was the Enforcer. By this time, Jack was running quicker in order to reach them before anything bad happened. He had seen this situation enough times to know what was going to happen next. The man picked up a rock and threw it at the Enforcer. The stone impacted the armour with a loud clank, but harmlessly bounced off. The stone had not even landed again when the Enforcer touched the man in the chest with a thick stick. A soft crackle was released and the victim fell to the ground, no longer cursing. His wife standing beside him was visibly horrified; her hands shaking and her thunderous eyes turning to the Enforcer. Jack wrestled her to the ground before she could make an attempt of revenge.

"Stop! Please," Jack yelled at the distraught woman while hugging her to prevent her from doing anything stupid, "You're only going to make things worse, please just calm down. You know the rules

Training aircraft overfly Green Area 1. These flights were critical for maintaining skills needed at the Exodus ship's destination.

of occupation are made for our benefit."

Jack continued soothing the woman until he felt her resistance slacken and she relaxed against him sobbing. When he felt that she was ready to think logically, Jack continued, "Your husband's going to be okay. He is just going to get some help for a while."

The woman nodded as if understanding, and Jack smiled, softly acknowledging her pain, "Now I want to take you and your son away from here, so we can get on with things. Do you think we can do it together?"

Again, she nodded and after picking up her bewildered child, Jack slowly took them to the exit. Jack looked back over his shoulder to see the Enforcer carefully pick up the unconscious man. After reassuring the broken family that everything was under control, Jack sent them on their way through the exit where stood another councilor Jack knew, who had been summoned by the Enforcer to help.

Jack returned to the lake and watched the Enforcer carry his human cargo away. The man would face disciplinary action and be required to undergo psychiatric care, so he could return to his duties soon. The man was lucky: his duties weren't essential for running the ship, so his re-education would be quicker than normal. Enforcement couldn't rick a reoccurring disobedience from essential personnel.

Nevertheless, Jack was lucky enough to be aboard one of the more advanced Exodus ships. Despite the craft's size and complexity, its repairs and routine functions were automated. However, everybody on board was gainfully employed to increase wellbeing on their craft, performing tasks as designed: non-repetitive and challenging, but, in the same time, quite useless from a safety perspective. Yet, this didn't give them an excuse to slack off as all work flows were closely monitored and any prolonged work reduction was swiftly and harshly dealt with by the Enforcement Team. Jack pitied the hundreds of other ships that had left with only a moment's notice, without any sort of planning. Their crews had probably already annihilated each other simply out of boredom. Most of those ships were little more than tin cans flying through space. They wouldn't be able to last a long time in space with no replacement parts to fix them for decades. Jack had no idea how many generations were needed to reach a habitable planet, even for their well-equipped Exodus.

He sighed and turned away from where the outbreak happened. Fortunately, public outbursts were few as most voyagers had learned to live in harmony within the provide life conditions. However, there were always individuals who would not accept this cohabitation status-quo and liked to push social barriers.

Of course, it had been much worse in the beginning of the trip. Then, the majority of the passengers found it impossible to have every move controlled and each action automated in order to prevent political upheavals in their tiny world. If not for the combined efforts of Jack and his fellow councilors, the entire Enforcement would have been destroyed by the distressed public. As it was, hundreds of people were sedated, and a few fire starters were dealt with in a more severe fashion. Jack still shivered at the memory of those dark days. Even he had trouble accepting that he couldn't help people be content since he had his own frustrations at times. Thankfully, the situation normalized and as years passed, babies were born on the ship, which helped the moral.

"Hello Jack!" A female voice broke into Jack's mind.

"Anna! Where are you off too?"

An attractive lady cycled next to him. She had come up from an adjacent track and was now keeping pace with him, smiling down from her lofty perch.

"Your pace is slowing, old man. You could just speed-walk you know." She let out a soft giggle.

"Anna, I see you have lost none of your charm or sarcasm! Your shift went well I take it?"

"Oh yes," Anna replied, "lovely time. Mind you, it's coming out here at the end of the day that makes me a lot happier."

"Couldn't agree more. Is the family out here with you as well?" Jack smiled, trying harder now to keep up with Anna's cycling.

"Only John, but I left him at his creche work for now, as I wanted a chance to ride a bit. And to see you!"

Jack laughed in response, "Thank you Anna! Is john going okay with his studies? The last time I saw him, he seemed a very bright boy."

Anna beamed, "Oh Jack, he's taking in all the training and still wants more. I really think he'll be the one…you know, when he's old enough, to…when we arrive…" Anna's bike wobbled.

Jack looked at her. Anna's face was furrowed, and she seemed on the verge of total apoplexy. He had seen the danger signals before and was ready for how to deal with it. Jack got Anna to stop and gently helped her dismount, holding her comfortingly.

Then he told her: "Johnny will be fine! He makes us all proud, you know that. And he'll do more… that day is coming! He is teaching these kids how to set up in a far off-world, you know."

Anna was gently crying now, "Yes, I know…I just…I'm a lot better now, really. I just need a little break now and then."

"That's okay," Jack replied positively. "I must say you've made great progress with your development! No wonder John does so well, I think I know where he gets it."

"You're such a smooth talker. Now I must get on my way or else John will think I've had a fall. Goodbye, Jack." Anna smiled brightly; her emotional lapse gone.

With grace, Anna remounted her bike and pedaled away, leaving Jack waving after her. He had known Anna for ten years; he first met her when she tried to kill herself. Her case was a sad one, like many others of that generation. She was a first comer, like Jack, one of the original passengers who had a previous life on Earth. Unlike Jack who had volunteered for service, Anna had been forced aboard the Exodus when her parents were declared rebels. She also came in with a twin brother Robby who died soon after, as he lacked the necessary medical assistance he needed for his chronic condition. Anna broke down during that time and was placed in psychiatric care, where Jack met her during his initial training. He played a major role in her development and was always pleased to meet her. John was also giving her hope for the future with his keen interest in the colorization training. And Jack knew that his friend was indeed worthy of being the first one to set foot on their distant home planet since he worked so hard to keep the spirts up on The Exodus.

Jack's chronograph sounded harshly. His time in 'Green Area 1' as about to expire, he sighed inwardly. He didn't even make it to Mt Pheasant; his stops to talk to the Enforcement Officer and Anna prevented him from doing so. Thankfully, he still had enough time to make it to the exits.

The rain began to trickle down as he was leaving. Smiling, Jack admitted to himself that he really enjoyed being on board of the Exodus, helping thousands of souls get along with their new lives. To be honest, he didn't really care if he would ever stand on a planet again; he just enjoyed his greenery, all 40 square kilometres of it allowed to him.

THE RESCUERS

(Above) The tranquil of Green Area 1 is shattered when a shuttle craft is hijacked in a desparate bid to get off the Exodus ship. The hastily-conducted plan meant that insufficient supplies could be gathered to ensure survival of the whole escape team.

The jungle world of Arkrane was one of the first exodus-related planets to be rediscovered. Most of its few hundred million exodus-born inhabitants resided in several megacities, leaving most of the lush forests and fresh water lakes to nature. This made Arkrane an absolute oasis for technology-weary tourists. Unfortunately, most would lose themselves in the many shopping precincts of these megacities.

Nevertheless, from time to time, some hundreds of visitors would leave civilisation behind to visit the remote Arkrane settlements. Fewer still would make the difficult trek to a centuries-old, corroded spacecraft, now part-buried in scrubby undergrowth and trees.

A simple stone memorial marked the site of this wreck. Its title in the native language said: "Mother".

Thump, thump, thump. The noise, amplified by the light-grade metal of the enclosure keeping out the vacuum of space, echoed loudly enough for almost everybody present to hear. Two teenage fists beat against the window frame in protest, as the girl, and dozens of others with her, physically or vocally expressed their displeasure at being confined in the small room. Those outside the room were almost as distraught, being forcibly removed from their fellows. They watched as dark squat shapes coaxed, pushed, pulled or manhandled the room occupants to a series of hatches leading to an assortment of spacecraft.

The minutes passed, the crowd inside the room dwindled, as they were forced into the transport craft. Suddenly alarms clamoured for attention, the area was bathed in red emergency lighting. People outside froze, then crushed forward to look through the space-grade glass separating them from those in the room. An accident had occurred; one of the transports had somehow come free of an airlock hatch. The inner room was now exposed to the vacuum of space. Those inside reacted noiselessly. Open mouths issued silent screams as the squat dark shapes tried unsuccessfully to reseal the hatch. As the room's precious atmosphere ebbed away, a young counsellor, turning his face away from the viewing window, thought he could hear a repeated noise reverberating through the frame. Thump, thump, thump.

Thump, thump, thump. The organic reclaimer announced the passing of another victim to the rest of the crew on its activation. The Reclaimer and the Terraformer craft it resided in screamed forward at ridiculous speed in the void of space in what had been planned as a fantastic rescue mission. However, things had not gone to plan and the nine original crew were down to six, and just now, five.

Lise sat with her other four rebels in the demoralising silence that had occurred four times before. At the start the plan had been simple. All of them had worked on the Exodus mothership and 'escaped' some time ago. Lise's original co-conspirator, Kyle, clattered the cards, snapping her mind to the recent past. The recent and final conversation the group had with its latest victim played in her head.

"I didn't ask for this," the man, whose name she could no longer remember, had complained. "We should not be doing this to each other".

"You know the rules; we all do," Kyle had said. "It is time to leave with honour for the program."

Lise did know the rules because she had helped invent them with the rest of the group.

Their stolen spacecraft was stuffed full of self-replicating micromachines and cryogenically frozen embryos to terraform a planet suitable for human life. Originally intended to land when the Exodus ship reached its destination, it had instead been stolen by the 'rescuers', as the original nine had called themselves. Their theory was simple: escape, set course to a suitable planetary system, stay fast asleep while the journey lasted and once the craft landed, be awoken by the automatic alarm to start a new life.

"It didn't quite work out that way," the victim had said. Coma-inducing injections induced life-threatening reactions and the deep-sleep capsules which were not configured properly in the rush to escape had killed one rescuer and almost another member of the group. But for the rescuers there was no return and no regret; they understood the risks and their present dire situation.

"Sigis was the lucky one, dying fast asleep," Lise said, wondering if she was right.

They had tried rostering between the few working sleep capsules, then started rationing, until inventing the game.

"It's simple enough," Kyle had said shuffling the cards. "When the supplies alarm goes off, each of us gets a card. The one with the keyed card leaves with honour for the program."

The one chosen to leave with honour had their body processed by the organic reclaimer in a bid to keep the remainder of the crew alive. The game was simple; it was keeping the rescuers alive in a devastating but efficient way. Three times the game had been played and each time the chosen one vanished both physically and from all future conversations. It was as if their existence had been erased.

Lise went along with the game, but hoped Kyle would be spared from drawing the card. She

(Above) The massive bulk of the Exodus ship slowly recedes in a viewing portal of the stolen terraforming craft. Most of those on board the terraformer faced a grim future in the vastness of space.

secretly hoped to start the new life with him by her side. That was what had got them off the Exodus ship in the first place. That, and a counselor called Jack.

Thump, thump, thump. Jack's shambling gait still made the too-thin ground reverberate hollowly. After all these years, Green Area 1 seemed unchanged. It still sprouted lush green grass, a fine mist drifted from above, and Lake Kannalis still glittered in the middle distance. The old Jack suddenly felt tired. Tired of the jog, tired of the grass, and the lake. His sight and hearing had improved, and his injured legs had almost completely been reconstructed.

A distant rumble rapidly grew in crescendo as one, now two, trainer craft streaked through the sky above him. If he looked carefully enough, he could almost tell there were fewer Enforcers here in Green Area 1 now. He smiled with the knowledge that maybe both of those things might just have been his fault, along with failure 432.

Years ago, now, Jack had just finished a counseling session when Lise and Kyle burst into his room.

"Did you hear? The system has gone down. Our infallible work program just crashed!"

Jack tried to feign ignorance: "Well you know the systems and work we do are only as good as the effort we, the workers, put into it. If things don't work well then we all need to reflect on what went wrong to work better next time."

"Rubbish," Kyle interjected. We're not in a counseling session now! I was flying the trainer when the avionics gave out, just like that!"

"You know that's never happened before," Lise said. If Kyle was not the best pilot in this place, he would not be here now!"

Jack was surprised that he had thought he could actually get away with lying to his two brightest students. Of course, he knew the work program had crashed, 431 times before in fact. This one, failure 432 must have been far worse to be able to disrupt a triply-redundant aircraft control system. Kyle started explaining in excruciating detail about his deftly performed manual control maneuvers, before Lise's sharp look cut him off.

"I was able to get into the back-door of the system while it was down, and I found what we have been looking for." Lise said.

Jack's eyes widened. Lise had committed a grievous crime, images of the teenager thumping fists against glass, a family being shocked into submission for overstaying in Green area 1, and other less pleasant punishments swam in his mind.

"Do you know what you have done?" Jack said. "I should report this – if the Enforcers don't already know about it already." Secretly Jack cared less about the enforcers than seeing his proteges in serious trouble.

"The system was down, remember?" Kyle interjected. "There was no surveillance from the Enforcers while we were on, we checked."

Jack, slightly mollified, asked them what they found, though in truth, he already knew.

The words spilled out of Lise: "First, it is all a fake, everything we do and work on is not needed. Our results and products disappear into the system and are never used for anything. Machines do everything for us, looking after all critical activities – you knew??"

Lise had reacted to Jack's expression. Jack decided to tell the truth. He explained the Exodus ship's work program's primary function was to keep its human occupants sane through the generations of travel time by giving them something meaningful to do. Time in the Green areas was carefully allotted to prevent burnout among the population.

The ruins of the Arkrane terraformer ship is becoming a popular destination for hardy outdoor trekkers.

Both Lise and Kyle deflated at learning their mentor had hidden this truth for them for so long. Kyle was the first to recover. "That was not all we found. This Exodus ship is meant to eventually take our future descendants to a habitable planetary system, right? We discovered that we have passed severable viable systems. We discovered this at about the same time that the records are showing that the Exodus population is shrinking."

At this Jack broke completely. Through his counseling work he had heard similar stories, and the pair's discoveries had confirmed his fears. Whether it was through the 432 system failures or something else, Exodus was steadily killing its people as its supplies dwindled. Perhaps the same failures also explained why Exodus appeared to be bypassing viable planetary systems.

Jack broke out of his revelry as he came up to Lake Kannalis. The conversation with Lise and Kyle was years ago now. He tried to push the memories out of his mind, but flashes kept returning. Jack used his influence to architect another system failure, where nine people would escape in a stolen shuttle designed to terraform. But three of them decided it was time to act. Over the coming months, the group had expanded to nearly 20.

Fearing discovery by the Enforcement, the group decided to enact Failure 433. Working the system so their times in Green Area 1 coincided, the group entered the artificial paradise. Six of the team, finding two family groups near Lake Kannalis, ran hard into them, bowling them over. Almost immediately Enforcers moved swiftly to the scene, while at the same time a fire broke out at the base of one of the environment control stations. Jack and the remainder of the team, taking advantage of the distractions, crowded into a blue and white trainer shuttle. Activating the controls, Kyle struggled with the overloaded craft as it blasted off to the transfer port where Lise knew a Terraformer ship awaited.

The shuttle made the journey in the confined Exodus craft in under two minutes. As Kyle struggled to land without killing them all, Jack hoped the systems outage caused by Failure 433 would be enough for them to transfer to the Terraformer and escape.

"Everybody out!" Lise ordered, as the shuttle crew picked themselves up from the hard landing. Nine had pressurised flight suits on, the shuttle's total compliment, while the rest, including Jack, had to go without. They pushed out of the shuttle hatch and made their way through a series of tunnels leading to the outside of the Exodus ship. Jack looked up, seeing the maze of supporting scaffolding that held up the imagined paradise of Green Area 1 just above their heads.

Courtesy of Failure 433, Kyle managed to open the transfer airlock and the team rushed inside – only to be met by five Enforcers waiting for them.

"How did they know?" one of the members started before an Enforcer silenced him with a touch of one of its appendages.

Kyle reacted immediately. He charged the Enforcers, hoping their flight suits might afford some protection against the Enforcers' weapons. Others followed after him, and for a moment it seemed to be working. Lise had accessed the Terraformer and some of the team were already making their way inside. Then, Jack felt his ears pop.

The Enforcers had decided to deal with the insurrection by opening the airlock to space. The cyclonic out rush of air sucked several of the team out into space in seconds. Three others were plucked from the hatch of the Terraformer.

For Jack, anchoring himself with airlock strapping, everything seemed to slow down. For some reason he gawked at how the light gleamed from the black armour of the Enforcers, the slow-motion movements of the doomed crew members cartwheeling end over end outside. He even had time to glance at Lise, grimly holding onto the Terraformer hatch restraint, before turning to the Enforcer at the airlock controls and jumping. The force of the tailwind caused Jack to bodily strike the Enforcer with enough force to snap his legs, and pitch them both into space.

Holding the faceless dark shape of his adversary in a death grip, Jack glimpsed the airlock closing, suited figures moving into the Terraformer. The next instant his eyes and lungs seemed to burn as gasses explosively left his body in the vacuum of intergalactic space. As his oxygen-deprived brain started to lose consciousness, Jack thought he had felt a violent thrust, and was now spinning toward the Exodus ship.

The old Jack stopped once again, coughing profusely. He had hobbled partway up Mt Pheasant to counsel a grieving parent. He had also forgotten his lungs and legs had never completely healed from the exposure to space all those years ago. Why had the Enforcer spared him, by hurling him back to the Exodus airlock? Even now memories of the months that followed the Terraformer escape eluded him. There were dim images of medical centres and painful rehabilitation but not much else.

He did know, thanks to Failure 433, that Exodus was back on track to reach a habitable system. Journey's end would happen far beyond his lifetime but he knew at least most of the descendants of Exodus would be alive to experience it. The routine on board Exodus was back to normal – records erasure, and his counselling efforts, had helped that process. Perhaps that was why he was rescued, to help life get back to normal. In the end, it didn't matter. Jack put those thoughts aside and prepared to do his job.

Lise, panted for breath as the smog-brown globe of the planet filled the Terraformer bridge windows. She was now the sole survivor, all except Kyle had sacrificed themselves for this planet. Lise refused to let Kyle take the 27 steps to the organic reclaimer. Instead they both chose to ration, then finally starve themselves. Kyle, slumped in the flight chair working course corrections for atmospheric entry, had died where he sat. Organic reclaimer nanoparticles, released by Kyle into the cockpit had efficiently and ruthlessly disassembled his body on sensing his death.

A rumble awoke a starved Lise, the Terraformer had entered the planet's atmosphere. Thump! The first Terraformer bomb automatically released into the upper atmosphere. The outgassed payload rapidly began to convert the brown smog to life protecting ozone.

Thump! The second bomb smashed into the stratosphere. Nanoparticles dispersed at hundreds of cubic metres a minute to create oxygen, swiftly spreading in the fast high-level winds.

Thump! The third and last bomb streaked through the lower atmosphere, raining water from hydrocarbons and leaving oxygen in its place.

Lise's oxygen-starved panting cured itself to normal breathing. For the first time, gasses from outside were being converted to life giving air in the cockpit, saving her life. She twisted the controls, her wasted arms fighting the ship into a semblance of smooth descent.

Hundreds of tons of terraforming technology, thousands of embryos and Lise finally came to rest in a shallow depression that was already filling with drinkable water. Above the cooling ship, the sky was already beginning to turn blue.

THE NEW START

(Above) Ancient Mars at its height rivalled Earth as a centre for advanced society and progressive thinkers. Its human-friendly environment was too fragile to survive the onslaught of the coming interstellar war.

Freya and Irs' colleague Phrane had just finished making camp near the 'Mother' wreck on Arkrane. Through their lobbying, the Terran and Irs government had provided additional help for Freya to continue investigating the period post-Exodus. Naturally this also meant undertaking educational field trips to many of the discovered Exodus worlds, including Arkrane.

"So you now think the 'rescuer expedition' to Arkrane was not really necessary?" Freya, moved by the shocking loss of life suffered by the Arkrane mission, asked incredulously.

Phrane was adamant. "You've been part of our Irs analysis, and you know our conclusions are well supported by evidence. The Exodus ship carrying Jack and the others actually survived to reach a habitable destination. Of course, they were only ten percent of the Exodus fleet that actually did so."

"And you think the planet they reached was Mortem, sister planet to the future Irs?"

Closing his eyes, Phrane could imagine what John, descendant of Anna, had experienced in the first landing on Mortem.

As his footsteps moved forward along the soft alien soil, John's lungs filled in with fresh air of the bizarre planet. The air didn't need processing or artificial scent. There was plenty of grass around too, but its natural green lining the ground had an artificial scent unlike the smell of natural fresh air surrounding him.

John smiled as he noticed that everyone aboard the transportation craft was making their way out into the open. Professional and disciplined people were acting like children again, and so they should, for it was extraordinary to be out in the open after their entire lives locked up in artificial environments. Like his colleagues, John had never known what it was like to walk on real soil, on uneven ground that prickles and scratches one's toes. Full of emotion, he looked once more at the blue sky: no ceiling trying to hide behind a make-believe haze, just pure, simple, blue infinity.

Phrane eventually replied. "The Exodus landers had established, probably using methods similar to ours, that Mortem was the only one in the system that bore a breathable atmosphere as well as an abundance of life. It became increasingly clear that humanity would not only be able to survive on that alien planet, but they would also be able to thrive in it."

Freya was still confused. "But if Mortem was such a good second home, then why bother to go to all the trouble of terraforming Irs?"

"Probably for the similar reasons that early Mars was terraformed during your home world's pre-history. Increasing the chances of survival of the people trying to settle that system, and possibly safeguarding against perceived Earth attacks are the leading theories at the moment."

Phrane was right about Mars, Freya thought. The Earth-like climate in which the pyramids and other ancient cities had been built was almost certainly artificial in origin. While she and Phrane were en-route to Arkrane, Freya's team had just discovered signs of earlier habitation, adapted for a much colder, drier Mars than had existed during the time of the pyramids.

Phrane continued. "The terraforming of Irs was much slower than for Arkrane, which as why it developed space travel much later in its history."

"Isn't it amazing that Earth and Irs, being so many light years distant, followed very similar paths in their societal development," Freya mused out loud.

"Like you, I'm amazed," replied Phrane. "Particularly given the vast variety of post-Exodus civilisations we keep discovering. The history of these other worlds is anything but similar; stories coming from these planets are bizarre indeed."

A PEEP THROUGH THE FOG

The Exodus cost society dearly, with hundreds of thousands of lives lost. Causes were many: critical malfunctions, collisions with uncharted debris or spacecraft simply drifting in endless space with crews starving as consumables ran out. Still others from the Exodus found alien worlds light years from Terra, developing societies far away from and unknown to their fellows. One such example occurred on an artificially created world called Segra.

The massive amount of work required to make Segra habitable took decades and eventually made its people quarrelsome, and mostly inhospitable people. Their principal talent became the ability to cultivate plants in the harshest of conditions.

Border pioneers eventually discovered Segra centuries after the Exodus, and many horticultural scientists were very interested in their heritage and work. Most of these requests were rebuffed, though a border patrol officer managed to venture within the Segran system. This is Captain Ricco's story.

***

There is no accounting for human taste. While Segran people praise their green valleys, I vividly remember their magnificent fog. Before I landed on Segra, I didn't pay attention to weather that much. As a pilot I have always appreciated good weather and clear, sunny days, but fog wasn't something I enjoyed. Even so, I found that the Segran fog is almost mystic, deep, intense and audacious. It comes out of nowhere and without any warning. Divine, rough, and glowing sombre, it behaves as an entity that somehow gets transfigured to follow you; creeping behind closed windows and sinking underwater. It gets inside your coat, under your collar, inside your hat – under your skin.

We had heard of the unfriendly nature of Segrans. Seeing us flying overhead, they would probably do what they could to evict us from their land. On this day we had lost our bearings in the fog and, suffering instrument problems, I and my copilot Oliver needed to land as soon as possible. The closest landing site was the farmer's paddock, but we had no idea that landing there was forbidden.

"Hey there! Stop!" yelled the farmer, whose name we later found out to be Mica, as we were on final landing approach. When he realised that we were not able to hear him, he started waving his arms into the air in a desperate effort to make us realise that he was serious about being left alone. But Oliver and I took no notice of him, concentrating on finding a dry patch to land. After circling his farm, we found a paddock of freshly harvested corn and maneuvered to skid close to each other. As we were shutting down, the farmer turned up, flushed as red as the crest of a rooster. He kept on shouting at us as he approached, trying to make us understand that he wanted us away from his farm.

"No outsider has ever dared to set foot on my land. Go away!" the farmer screamed while waving a rake at us. We took our helmets off, tried to say hello to the man, but he seemed in no mood for introductions. He flatly refused to even let us know where we were. Then suddenly a fog dropped out of nowhere and hid the farmer from our sight. Space seemed frozen in time. While this was happening, we temporarily forgot about the annoying farmer for a while. When the fog lifted, he had given up yelling and seemed to calm down.

I tried talking to him again: "Hey Mica, is there anywhere we could go to get a cup of water?" I said politely.

"Yes, in the ditch down near the water tank, over there," replied a less grumpy Mica.

"Ok, we can try that," Oliver added in a low voice. I agreed. As we descended from our craft to depart, Mica cried out: "You can't leave your equipment here!"

(Preceding page) The artificially created and bizarre environment of Segra was home to a population of equally bizarre rural cultivators. Visitors to Segra were definitely not welcome and low-level overflights, such as illustrated here, carried a degree of risk.

"And what exactly do you suggest we do?' Oliver asked, exasperated. "Put our planes onto our backs and drag them into the ditch?"

"'Suits me fine," Mica retorted. "But make sure you don't disturb soil! My crops need perfectly aligned rows!"

I tried to reason with him. "Listen, Mica, we can't do anything without help. And the longer you plan to delay us in getting help, the longer we'll stay on your land. The minute the rest of this fog clears away, we can get away from here."

"The fog clearing? You're joking, right? Don't you know…" the farmer broke off chuckling.

"What are you trying to say?" I worried. "That we might be stuck here in the fog with you?"

"Maybe so," Mica continued without giving any more clues.

"Stop all this nonsense and take us inside to call for some help," Oliver cut in. "Surely, you can see that our request is reasonable and we can remunerate you greatly when all this is over."

Finally, Mica relented, directing us to a small path to follow. Beckoning us to his cabin, he warned us not to make ourselves too comfortable.

I started to think that maybe this strange land with its oppressive fog might have affected these people... Or maybe I was dreaming; the man could have simply been strange, so isolated from others that he forgot the meaning of hospitality.

Since Mica was leading the way, I couldn't stop admiring the view through breaks in the fog. In the distance the Segran city towers were massive, and the vegetation all around us looked so green and the air so fresh. I tried to touch a corn but, as I did, the wind blew it away, and for some reason I thought this strange. The corn almost seemed to pull away from me. I had no time to investigate as I was following the farmer, trotting carefully in Oliver's footsteps. It thought it might be the fog making me see things that weren't possible.

Soon enough we reached the top of a small hill, staring at a well-kept wooden cabin. Its windows were large and beautifully decorated with flowers under their seals.

When we entered the cabin, we both liked its cosiness and couldn't help admiring the furniture, which perfectly matched the dark brown wood panels.

I couldn't see outside as the fog had thickened, wrapping around each window. But this did not matter as I was keen to have a warm drink and find out more about where we were.

"Thank you for your hospitality," I said while warming my hands on the drink.

"Never mind, I am glad you like it here. I like it too. Foolish of me to try to leave this place some years ago…but that's all in the past now." a nicer Mica confessed.

"Why? What happened?" I asked.

But the farmer cut his own story off, instead changing the subject to why we were here. Oliver, trying to maintain good relationships, went on to explain our survey role, and that somehow, we had lost contact with our fleet and needed to land.

"Yes, we were quite lucky to land here...just as our controls began to fail." continued Oliver.

Even more surprisingly Mica offered the use of his communication system. He pointed to an old rusty box in the corner of his kitchen. We gladly accepted and reached for the equipment which, despite its age was still in good working order. Oliver excitedly keyed the pilot in distress signal, but there was no answer at the other end. I thought that was strange and blamed the fog.

"Yes, it must be the fog, by this time the wind currents have dragged it high into the sky by now," agreed Mica. What he said seemed true because we could now clearly see the beautiful green patches of corn and our beleaguered craft in the distance.

In a strange way we were glad. While I was trying to reach my survey fleet, Oliver put on his boots and decided to go for a walk to enjoy this paradise view while he could.

As he was walking down the narrow path, he noticed the yellowish substance at the root of each corn plant. "Horrible gluey stuff. It's funny that it smells so good but…" Oliver told himself as he looked up to admire the multicoloured butterflies and parrots overhead.

Soon he found a small hole in the ground and idly wondered what animal could live inside it. As he was trying to get a better look, his left foot slipped, splashing the yellowish substance on his boots and ankles. Through the window I saw him scrape some soil and rub it on the yellowish material to make the stickiness go away. He changed his mind and stopped looking for whatever animal was hiding underground. As he swirled around, he noticed that the corn plants which were growing a couple of meters away seemed much closer. He wiped the sweat of his forehead and took a small step to return back to the cabin. However, he couldn't find the path back. It was if it had vanished. He must have been very tired and confused, so he retraced his steps to have a better look. Eventually he was able to see the path again, which gave him great relief; getting lost once that day was enough for him.

As he was making his slow progress up the hill, he, like me, was fascinated by the deep green plants, and by what had happened when tried to touch the corn. The branches pulled back and he knew immediately that this kind of behaviour wasn't normal for a plant. He tried again and again but got frustrated from the illogical behaviour of the plant. He had gotten ever closer to the root and though he felt disgusted at having to step into the yellowish gluey secretion, he did it in order to grab the plant. He immediately felt an electric shock and his hand let go of the plant. Then, a pain in his knees made him look down and he saw that there was blood where the yellow stuff had touched his skin. His boots were partially destroyed from small holes as if they were burnt.

He didn't like this farm any more. Despite its beautiful views, nice smells and lovely bird songs, he wanted to get away from such extravagant flora and fauna. He decided to quicken his step and call out for me: "Hey Ricco, can you come out?"

I heard his voice and stepped outside to see what my friend wanted.

"What's up, Oliver?" I had finally got in contact with my team and was just about to provide coordinates to them. I quickly ducked back into the doorway to complete my transmission when I heard an anguished scream.

I knew instantly that the voice was Oliver's so I rushed outside. As I was trying to run quickly, I stumbled on something and started rolling down the path until my feet hit something hard; Oliver's boots. They looked terribly damaged.

There was no sign of Oliver himself, and I started to panic. It seemed as if the ground had swallowed him up.

I decided that the paddock was not safe for me so I got up and ran as fast as I could into the cabin and closed the door after me. Finding Mica, I started grabbing him, to take him out the door with me to search for my copilot.

The farmer slowly turned and looked at me as if I said something stupid. Then, pointing to the corn fields, he said in a whispering voice: "It's those plants…from time to time they have to have their way."

"What do you mean?" I asked, extremely worried.

"Can't say more. That's it. There is nothing you can do! Just leave him!" he advised.

"What do you mean? Is there a way to protect ourselves? What haven't you told me?" I barked angrily.

"You would have not believed me!" Mica said as if amused. He turned away, clearly not willing to continue the conversation. I went the other way, trying the communications equipment again to send the critical coordinates for our rescue.

I had just sent the coordinates when Mica, who had been doing something at the back of the cabin, returned with a plate of steaming corn.

"Better have this!" he said enigmatically.

I didn't know what to do. Will he try to poison me? What did he do to my friend? "Is it safe?" I managed to add swallowing as quietly as I could so he couldn't see my fear.

"Well I think it is better than what will come if you refuse!" Mica said briefly, in his characteristic short speech.

Pretending to be braver than I actually felt, I had a small bite and then another one and soon, the cob was finished. I was waiting to die any minute, but nothing happened. So, I didn't get the mystery of Mica's advice.

Luckily, he continued soon after. "Well done, you are safe now. The plant eats you or you eat it… nothing in between. Better remember that!" Mica said very quietly.

"What? What's this? Are you playing tricks with me?" I asked him.

"No, that's the way it goes around here. And you are lucky I told you."

I had enough. Seeing no value in continuing the conversation and not bothering to thank my host for the meal. I wanted to find my copilot, I wanted off this rock and could not get out of Mica's cabin fast enough. The farmer muttered something inaudible behind my back that was not exactly friendly.

As I was walking down the path again, I left very uncomfortable seeing the branches of vegetation move away from me. I have since learned that this was real, they were really plants behaving like people. It was almost as if they liked to be admired and flattered as they bowed before me while I passed, admiring them.

My thoughts changed to Oliver, still missing. I thought about the sticky, yellowish substance at the corn's roots, even now steaming with vapour that seemed to be mixing with a suddenly darkening purple fog. Before I knew it, every plant in range started shaking wildly, slashing at my feet and ankles.

I instinctively stepped back off the path, too late realising I was surrounded by hundreds of slashing cornstalks. I tried to run, then was swallowed up by the putrefied yellowish secretion, falling amongst ever cutting plants. Just before I was overwhelmed, I screamed "STOP!"

Suddenly, it was all over. Somehow, I was driven forward and found myself back on the path, struggling for breath. The corn had let me go, and as the purple fog began to clear once again, the farmer's field began to look once again like an ordinary field of corn plants. I had no idea how I escaped, and my legs seemed to have a will of their own, running on until I had reached the safety of our craft.

As I fumbled to open the canopy door, I did not dare to look back, or even think about poor Oliver, still out somewhere in the corn that was not corn. Was he alive or dead? I did not even allow myself time to think – I leaped into the cockpit and locked the latch behind me.

I don't know how long I was there, but when I opened my eyes again, I was in the sickbay on the primary survey ship, being attended to by medical orderlies. I could barely see Segra out the window, by now a bright star among many bright stars as the survey team departed the system.

It was some time before I recovered. I remember the medical staff telling me that I had been under the influence of powerful hallucinogens. Preliminary testing by the team's science section showed that these seemed prevalent in the entire Segran ecology, with effects that increased with exposure. As such, the team that rescued me were unable to spend much time looking for Oliver. As it was, two of the rescuers were also badly affected, prematurely ending the recovery efforts. I was told that if I hadn't locked myself in the artificial atmosphere of my landing craft when I did, I would have shared the same fate as my fallen colleague.

None of the returned recovery team mentioned anything about the farmer Mica or his cabin – had I imagined the whole thing? If so, then whose equipment did I use to make the distress signal? A detailed on-orbit remote mapping and search activity was started to try and locate Oliver; however the unpredictable fog plus mysterious technical glitches in the fleet forced an early suspension of the activity. Fearing critical system failures, the survey team elected to leave while they could, leaving behind a hazardous environment beacon to warn any future unsuspecting craft of the dangers of the Segra system.

***

Oliver was listed as 'missing on duty' and Ricco was eventually reassigned to other duties. Subsequent robotic and manned outreach missions to the Segran system fared no better than Ricco's survey team, making certification of his version of events impossible.

(Above) A survey team beats a hasty exist from the Segra surface. Many aboard the survey ship could not leave the planet fast enough, leading to the system being designated as a restricted area.

THE END OF NIGHT

(Above) The cold wastelands of Alda II, with the dormant star that Rita and her team struggled to bring back to life. Much of the ground ice was found to be frozen atmospheric material that supported a more hospitable environment before Alda II's star lost brightness.

After the crash landing of their particular Exodus craft on a dark planet, Alda II, the four remaining survivors tried to save themselves by reactivating the system's dead star. Resources and consumables running low, the group of top professionals were running out of time…

Star Matter expert Yves, Nuclear Physicist Bruno, Biochemist Alyssa and Rocket Engineer Rita were optimistic that their latest experiment would work. They had successfully given birth to a 3 cm diameter 'star' inside their temporary rock-ice cave shelter. Now they only needed to scale the experiment up a million-fold.

Rita fingered a small jar of exotic material between her fingers. "How great it would be to be able to fall asleep" she confessed out loud. She was not resting well, not for a while now. She was alone, her lab was deserted. A scale-up attempt had gone quite wrong, and now the new rule was complete isolation for whoever was actually running the experiment. Some days ago, she thought he had to reach a solution to rekindle the dead stellar fires, but now, she was no longer sure. What if the 'magic formula' to save their lives was just words scribbled on her screen and nothing more. She felt like her years of career expertise would be worthless, even though the key stakes were for survival.

Where were the others? Surely, with no actual experimentation going on there should be at least one person around to talk to. Rita tried to think how long it had been since she started the scale-up version 2: two days? A week? Fatigue coursed through her again. She was so tired…

Not that long ago, everything was going smoothly as they were indeed making great progress with their research in restarting the system's star. Rita and the others launched a probe into Alda, with the exotic matter of her own concoction producing encouraging bursts of energy. They celebrated their first victory by consuming a week's worth of rations under the already fading glow of Alda's glare.

Inspired, Bruno also worked his own experiment, aiming to make the reaction last longer. Compressing millions of years of natural evolution into a few hours, Bruno led the group to create the stable, 3 cm star in the depths of their ice cave. While Bruno took the credit, Yves, Alyssa and Rita spent the next two semi-drunken hours of the second celebration arguing with him that it was a team effort. All of them had discovered or used parts of the environment around them to help create the stable reaction.

Where were the rest of the team? Rita shivered coldly, despite the artificial environment. There seemed to be an aura of bad energy surrounding their darkened cave, along with its smaller darkened tunnels trailing away to endless destinations beneath the planet's ice. The professional skeptic within her shrugged off such silly thoughts. She reasoned a rational explanation for her mood. In amongst their frantic stellar experiments, the team, scurrying through the caves to find this material or connect that equipment had found some additional discoveries. A super-excited Yves announced the first discovery – ordered markings on part of the cave walls made by a long-gone intelligence. Crude but effective translations of the writings spoke of a society living under a bright Alda sun. Part-buried artefacts from these beings were also observed for the first time, scattered on the icy surface around their cave.

Rita remembered how, after the initial excitement, the mood of the team suddenly changed. Alyssia's biochemist-fuelled babble about past life forms flourishing, then vanishing under a darkening sun, were silenced by Bruno and Yves. Survival was the priority they argued; the team had no time for frivolous activities such as extra-archaeology. Their reasoning was sound, but Rita wondered if in fact the mood changed because the translated writings had labelled their area as 'Cemetery Cave'. Did anyone really want to go on exploring to find out what happened to the Aldarians, particularly in Cemetery Cave?

The team's logical minds publicly dismissed thoughts of previous dwellers going mad in this cave, turning on each other for dwindling resources before finally freezing to death. Privately though, Rita noticed that none of the team, herself included, were too keen to dig too deep or venture further into the cave than was absolutely necessary to finish their experiments. There were also the small but niggling accidents that had happened over the past few weeks.

Shaking her head, she put it all behind her, telling herself that they have just had several misfortunes which are common to all scientific expeditions. Rita told herself she was more successful than both Yves and Bruno put together. It was her idea to send the probe to Alda and her idea of initiating the stellar reaction that temporarily brightened the star. It was true that her decisions were hard to decrypt and her occasional outbursts of anger sometimes kept the team on edge, but she always had good results.

After the second experiment, the accidents started happening. Bruno had prematurely shut off the tiny star experiment, causing a temporary power outage in their laboratory. Yves had accidently irradiated himself from a too-rushed experiment and commenced to complain about the dwindling state of the rations. Alyssa, feelings still hurt from the previous life-form episode, was eating some warm fish in the kitchen. Yves suddenly announced fish make him sick as they remind him of the yellowish water that seeped from the cave walls. He also advised Alyssa and that she shouldn't be eating so much anyway, given the state of the rations. Alyssa was put off her food, and left for bed.

Both Bruno and Rita cornered Yves for a short but harsh chat, and eventually the humbled scientist made his way to bed. Trying to sleep, he imagined a fish, fastened upside down by a large hook on one of the cave walls. That made him sick, and he raced up to the bathroom. His feet slipped on something, and he looked down to see he had stepped on a smelly fish from the ration stores. Now half-mad with nausea, Yves rushed forward, only to slip again. He was impaled on a metal protrusion that—to his dying brain—seemed like a giant fish hook.

Rita remembered the next morning being a hard time for the remaining three scientists following the grisly discovery. Was it an accident or had Yves been deliberately killed? Hasty investigations found nothing, so they decided to keep on working, for time was precious.

For the next several days they worked hard, celebrating with drinks after another breakthrough. Bruno announced he needed to go lie down as his eyes were smarting. Rita grunted at his retreating back that he should stay a bit longer, since they were planning to do the quick recap on how to proceed for the next experiment.

Bruno's burning eyes persisted through the morning, and to Rita's annoyance, Alyssa now had to spend increasing amounts of time trying to treat the nuclear physicist, taking her away from her work. Rita, as always, was very determined to complete their task. She was sure they were near to reactivating Alda, and paid no attention to the suffering Bruno.

It was about this time, she remembered, that she lost track of time. She couldn't remember much of the days that followed, only that Bruno's condition steadily got worse until he too was placed beside his fallen colleague Yves, in a disused side-tunnel of the cave.

"Maybe Bruno had touched the exotic matter or contaminated his eyes somehow," Rita had told Alyssa.

"No one is to blame but this cursed cave," she continued as if she was talking to herself. Alyssa, said nothing, there was nothing more for her to add – words were useless. They both knew they were soon about to be dead as well - if the Alda sun wasn't going to be reignited soon.

More delicate and less obstinate to get quick results, Alyssa looked very closely at her friend's body and concluded that there was little she could have done to save him. She found it strange that Bruno had been so careless with the extremely hazardous exotic matter. But then, who could have been his enemy? She and Rita had needed his help, particularly with preparing for their evacuation. Reigniting Alda would give them all the energy they needed, - but temporarily make Alda II uninhabitable. Bruno had split his time between the stellar reactivation testing and preparing an escape ship where they could depart from, and return to, Alda II once the initial radiation surge had passed.

Alyssa, wondering who might be the next to die, started taking advantage of Rita's work obsession. She increasingly absented herself to continue the late Bruno's work on the escape craft. The self-absorbed Rita barely noticed her companion's absence; working for days to prepare, then debug the final stellar reactivation. She had a vague recollection of a journal taken from Alyssa's quarters, she could not remember when or why. Absently Rita had flipped through the pages, discovering her companion's suspicions about the two deaths.

Within the diary's pages, Rita found no logical explanation for Alyssa's mistrust of her. It had been very hard for her to accept that behaviour from such a quiet colleague like Alyssa. But Alyssa had doubted her and that still hurt.

A muffled report roused Rita from her musings for a few moments, before she returned to her work.

"Poor Alyssa," Rita said softly to herself as fragments of her colleague fell like snow just outside the cave. Rita couldn't say with certainty what Alyssa had been planning, but a well-placed explosive charge activated when her colleague passed nearby settled the matter once and for all.

Rita, sole survivor, denying any connection to human beings apart from accepting their help to complete her own mission, prepared to leave. As inscrutable as her way of seeing people, she began her travel into the night towards the unknown.

A blinding flash brought her to the present. Sometime she had fallen asleep through strange murmurs and flitting shadows of her own consciousness. Her experiment had worked! Alda had reignited, illuminating her retreating spacecraft and the recently departed planet, far below. The high-energy wave rapidly dissipating, Rita prepared to turn her ship around and return to an already warming Alda II. Would the ancient Aldarians return to their restored home? She pondered these as she keyed up the mission return sequence to get back.

Sparks, blue smoke and sharp explosions were all that greeted her efforts. Rita was plunged into darkness, the power system cutting out through a cascading series of shorts. She screamed, flying into a fit as an all-too familiar tool floated out from behind the control panel. "Alyssa!" she shrieked as she realised her dead colleague, understanding the psychopath Rita was, had made sure there would be no return to Alda II.

The powerless ship continued to fly away from the system, slowly choking the life of its sole occupant. Rita struggled to get a better view of that now colourful planet she was leaving further behind. For a moment the stars around her promised magic and light. Then, darkness followed. She died as she wished: alone and unnoticed.

(Above) Propellant and other consumables exhausted, Rita's lifeless ship drifts away from the newly-reactivated Alda II star. The planet itself was rediscovered recently, with efforts underway to restore its previously-frozen ecosystem.

WHAT YOU BRING WITH YOU

(Above) The presence of an abandoned but perfectly functional lander in the Hercules system perplexed a subsequent rescue team. A critically ill crew member was all the rescue team could find of the original mission.

The origins of the rusting craft, the first indications that humanity was not alone, remained a mystery for some time. Its story began in the century following the Exodus.

Pegasus: …"Ok Morpheus, we're all back inside. We're a little tired. Those deployable kits were a bear to set up, but the procedures went really well."

Morpheus: "Pegasus we copy you are back inside and that the EVA was nominal?"

Pegasus: "It sure was Morpheus, we had a little trouble with … Charlie Bus spiking into the auxiliary node … good enough to continue and we're ready for close-out."

Morpheus: "Pegasus, those coms dropouts seem to be back in force but we're reaching the end of our telemetry pass anyway. We really enjoyed the show up here, and congratulations on a great first day."

Pegasus: "Roger that Morpheus, we're very excited to be here and can't wait to start the real work tomorrow. The only way is up…"

I can clearly remember that last exchange between Morpheus and Pegasus. In fact, it is about the last thing I can clearly remember about that mission. I am otherwise floating in a dark void. Flashes of indistinct light illuminate an indistinct environment like distant lightning through cloud. A thin, endless strand rises above my dark horizon and passes soundlessly overhead. Revealing a double helix structure. DNA, a distant voice seems to say, then the darkness returns.

I remember the Morpheus mission clearly enough, having been one of the EVA crew of the Pegasus lander. Our team were the absolute best - hand selected from thousands of top-line pilots, scientists and engineers, to travel further than any mission before us. We had all trained most of our adult lives for what was advertised as a very deep space journey. The mission itself could easily be described in just a few words: travel to an extrasolar planetary system where indications of life had been detected, land to set up a staging post, then await a relief crew. The preparation, development and undertaking of the mission of course took much longer.

Morpheus, a 300 m long starship capable of travelling the vast distances between solar systems, was the pinnacle of a series of increasingly sophisticated space missions. She was to carry all the equipment, two landers, and a crew of 10 across the many light years between home and Herculis, the system where extra-terrestrial life was thought to exist.

Deep space robotics surveys had confirmed the existence of a gas giant and smaller planets around the G-type Herculis star, though none of these worlds had generated much interest outside astronomical circles. Two of the Herculis moons, however, briefly stopped day-to-day activities across humanity. These moons were found to offer the best chances of finding evidence of intelligent life outside our solar system. Bio markers, and strong evidence of metallic structures had been detected, and Morpheus, the end product of a new 'star race' had been born.

Commander Eli James led the Pegasus team that had departed for Herculis 2 on Morpheus's long-awaited arrival, at the distant star system. I accompanied our five-person crew as lead biologist, and like all of us, could not wait to earn our pay on the ground.

Currently floating in this never region, I find it hard to remember how excited we were about the mission. The landing had gone so well as to be almost routine. Eli expertly piloted Pegasus through Herculis 2's thin atmosphere, and apart from occasionally monitoring lander systems, the rest of us were treated to an alien sun illuminating a multicoloured alien landscape below us. Signs of life were almost everywhere. The little moon, stretched and squashed by a complex interplay between the Herculis planet and third moon, Hercules 3, sported thousands of hot-water-filled crater lakes. Skirting each shimmering water body like bath-tub rings was a multi-coloured display of algal and lichen plants. Each sported a colour in response to temperature changes between the hot water and the cooler parts of the crater walls.

As Pegasus settled to land, we were striving to find the real reason that brought us out here, the supposed artificial structures. None of us had seen them from the remote sensing done by Morpheus, or the closer views from the descending Pegasus. But Ethan, our technical expert, was sure they existed. Something had been plaguing our communications with Morpheus, to the point that Eli had to do the landing pretty much without backup telemetry from the mother craft. Eli did get us down though, and enough of a message was received by Morpheus to know we were safe.

For the next 36 hours the whole lander team was extremely busy completing post-landing checks and conducting our first EVA to set up equipment needed to sustain us on the surface. Unofficially, we were also racing the team of the second lander mission, Odyssey. They were due to fly to the Herculis 3 moon when their launch window opened in a about a fortnight. We of the Pegasus team wanted to be the first to discover intelligent alien life, and we were already winning by being the first to land.

Small technical problems had delayed our equipment fit out and testing, and we were running short on communications time back to Morpheus. As it was, the tired but exhilarated Eli's last message to Morpheus was cut short: "Roger that Morpheus, we're very excited to be here and can't wait to start the real work tomorrow. The only way is up…"

Pegasus was never heard from again.

At first the Morpheus crew were unconcerned. The premature termination of the transmission was only a few seconds short of the end of the coms pass, and was put down to the interference that had plagued the mission so far. Returned telemetry from the lander up to that point showed a healthy spacecraft so the Morpheus team were not overly worried about a few seconds of lost coms.

The real worry began at the next scheduled pass. The casual language of "Good Morning Pegasus, rise and shine," soon gave way to curt: "Pegasus, Morpheus," as the Morpheus team tried to raise our surface crew. The landing logs and telemetry files were examined repetitively, processed by the mothership's computer system to find any anomaly that could explain the extended outage. As before, returned telemetry from the lander showed a healthy spacecraft, with plenty of consumables available to sustain the landing team for an extended period. These facts were argued extensively by the remaining Morpheus crew for days after the last transmission, as the 'best of the best' continued to try and solve what had gone wrong.

By the fourth day, Dylan Thomas, the Morpheus Executive Officer, was forced to make a decision. Along with the Pegasus anomaly, Morpheus itself began to experience problems. Kyrsten, systems modeler, had alerted the Morpheus crew to the problem two days earlier.

"The propellant containment system is fluctuating and draining power. We need to cut our mission short."

This had generated fresh tension with the team. Having just got there, no one was in a hurry to return home again, especially with Pegasus missing.

"Maybe the Morpheus build was too rushed; perhaps the engine and drive system is still too new," theorised Kyrsten and other members. If I had been in a condition to care, I would have sympathised with Dylan. Missing out on the coveted commander position by only a small percentage, the executive officer was a capable leader in his own right. Not only was he relegated to second place after Eli, he was burdened with breaking the bad news to the home worlds. Morpheus, the exemplar very deep space mission was in trouble, and its prime lander team was out of contact. It was also up to Dylan to decide what to do next.

The several day's delay had allowed a second launch window to the Herculis 2 moon to open up, and the hastily reassigned Odyssey lander team was sent to the surface to discover the fate of Pegasus. Notably absent from the Odyssey crew, was Dylan, who, almost to the point of insubordination, was forcibly censured by Earth and the rest of the Morpheus team to remain on board the mothership. It would not do to lose two commanders in as many weeks.

Odyssey's crew were treated to the same stunning vistas as their predecessors a week earlier. Somehow though the rainbow-coloured lichen rings and deep crater appeared more ominous to the lander team. An unspeakable danger seemed to encompass Odyssey as the little lander made the second ever landing on this alien moon.

Like the Pegasus team, the Odyssey crew raced against the clock to conduct their mission. Unlike our earlier team, Odyssey were not looking to 'be the first' but were instead racing against hard deadlines of a closing launch window, and the declining ability of Morpheus to get them home again.

"Ok you need to slow down and think the process through," Dylan admonished from above as a member almost left the lander without sealed pressure suit.

"I appreciate your urgency but we need to do this right. Find the team, come back to us. That's all I ask."

Despite the mishap, the Odyssey EVA proceeded as planned, driving the short distance between their lander and the Pegasus ship. As the crew approached the first landing site, they saw nothing out of the ordinary. Departing their rover, they walked past numerous deployable equipment, all in seeming working order. The Pegasus lander appeared pristine, though the outer hatch was wide open. Standard EVA procedure normally called for closing this hatch to protect the airlock from alien weather events.

Three of the crew gained access to the interior of Pegasus, manually resetting the airlock and moving into the darkened interior. Suit head lamps were turned off as Kyrsten brought Pegasus's interior lighting and other systems back online.

"Everything here appears nominal, power levels, flight software, everything," transmitted Kyrsten to the Morpheus crew from the Pegasus lander after an initial system check.

"Copy that Odyssey," replied Dylan breaking through the ever-present communications dropouts.

"I won't remind you of the tight deadlines we have here so please begin your Pegasus close-outs and prepare for the next phase of the schedule."

A distressed Kyrsten realised she could do no more inside the lander. Data logs were hastily copied from Pegasus, and the crew departed the lander to return to Odyssey. As Pegasus shrank behind the rover, the team puzzled over what they had found, or what they didn't find. They had left a perfectly working spacecraft that theoretically could return to Morpheus at any time. The rebooted systems were now broadcasting a directional beacon to the still missing crew and returning healthy telemetry back to Morpheus.

The second and last day on Herculis 2 dawned with Odyssey already on the surface, driving around in a search of the missing crew. Dylan knew they were pushing themselves past accepted safety margins, but could not delay their mission. Morpheus was still misbehaving and declining energy levels had placed a hard stop on their departure date from the system.

Odyssey used state of the art mini drones, grid searching and team splitting to scour tens of kilometres of Herculis 2. They ignored the fantastically colourful lichen-covered crater lakes and even objects looking vaguely artificial as they traversed the terrain, avoided obstacles and crunched the drone data. Twice the Pegasus rover team swerved to avoid half-hidden rover-swallowing holes or wheel-crushing boulders.

The shrunken Herculis star was sinking in the moon's sky when Odyssey received the call they had hoped not to hear.

"Ok Odyssey, commence your close-out procedures, it's time to come home."

Dylan had agonised over making the call to bring the team back, deliberately allowing the pre-determined deadline to expire. Now he could wait no longer.

"We're not done yet; we're driving in circles and getting nowhere," Kyrsten had shot back.

"This is not up for debate Odyssey. You are running out of light and are low on rover power. Scrub the EVA," responded a sympathetic but firm Dylan.

"We are not done yet," Kyrsten said softly to herself as she nonetheless prepared to drive home. By chance, her team's rover was the furthest out, in a rockier portion of the moon upslope of the crater lakes. Exceeding the rover drive limits by an excessive margin, Kyrsten drove in a wide arc over unexplored terrain, to maximise the chance of exploring a few more square metres of ground.

It was this last action that allowed her team to find me.

I was lying face down in my pressure suit, several kilometres from Pegasus, with no clear explanation as to how I got there or why I was in that particular location. I was in no condition to answer; my suit had run out of oxygen and I was in a deep coma from hypoxia.

Kyrsten's call for a mission extension were rejected, and after plugging in emergency purge oxygen to my life support system, her team bundled my up to the rover and steered back to Odyssey.

I remained comfortably oblivious to all that occurred around me in the days, weeks and months that followed my discovery. Hastily stripped of all that wasn't needed to keep us alive for the trip some, the Odyssey ascent stage had lifted off as planned and returned to Morpheus. If any Pegasus crew should return to our landing site, they would find enough supplies to keep three times their number alive on Herculis 2 for years.

The Morpheus team returned safely to our home world, with me kept alive by the on board medical equipment, though Dylan fared worse off than his ailing mothership. Official enquiries cleared the Executive Officer of any negligence, and praised his efforts for safely coming home. Unofficially though, he was forever marked as the leader who abandoned a third of his team to an unknown fate, light years from home. On my return I was transferred to a neural rehabilitation unit on request of Kyrsten and others of the Morpheus team. Brain damage was extensive, they were told, and increasingly experimental procedures were suggested by increasingly unstable ex-astronaut Dylan, to recover my memories for what happened to Pegasus.

My floating darkness occasionally lifts, bursts of light struggle to shine through the darkness. Very occasionally, incoherent light forms a brief image of a friend. Eli flashed into view, slowly turning towards me while at the same time he collapsed in on himself, exploding into millions of DNA fragments. Kyrstin, grimly steering her rover, dawned on my consciousness, condemned to drive in circles until she too disappeared in a cloud of DNA strands.

The experimental treatment slowly rebuilt my mind, and the Morpheus Mystery faded from the public consciousness as other life-bearing worlds were found and other space heroes pushed ever further to exploit them. Life was precious, and extrasolar worlds containing the ingredients to support biology were crucial in sustaining the generations of humanity after the exodus a century before. Had this extra-terrestrial life been seeded in strategic locations for our benefit and continued survival? Were these signs of biology evidence for a long-past experiment to make the building blocks for oasis of humanity in space? Answering these questions was part of the justification for very deep space missions such as Morpheus.

While Morpheus faded into history, the mission became ever clearer in my healing memory. A slowly brightening light began to rim the horizons of my ever-present darkness. Fragments of the Pegasus landing began to persist in my mind: the glorious views, Eli's soft touchdown and the endless unpacking of stores.

"His brain activity has spiked in the last hour," a disembodied voice rose from the dark, then was replaced by a furtive climb down the Pegasus ladder in alien darkness, and then an explosion of DNA strands. The light gathered on my horizon of darkness. I saw again Eli piloting Pegasus to a safe landing, the multicoloured crater lakes, the unpacking of stores.

Sometime later, I don't know when, I woke up. A beaming Dylan was smiling down at me. My long-unused jaws struggled to speak. "Dylan, how long has it been?"

My former executive officer didn't answer, he just continued to smile that enigmatic smile. "Did you find the rest of the team?" I asked my rescuer. Dylan simply smiled, while a smiling Kyrstin stepped out from behind him. I thought she had stepped forward; though to my just recovered mind, she seemed to just appear from behind Dylan. Impossible of course.

"Kyrstin, how did you get here? Did you find us all?"

Without answering, Kyrstin shared the same smile as Dylan. Behind her, Eli, my old commander, appeared from behind. I couldn't contain myself. With surprising strength given my extended time in a coma, I rose out of my medical bed to give them a hearty embrace. It was then that I glimpsed a multicoloured crater lake passing behind a nearby window. I stopped mid-action, realising that somehow, I was on the Morpheus.

"What is this? Did we never leave" What is going on?" I couldn't contain myself. A featureless, black cliff began to form on the horizon of my mind, gradually edging closer.

The smiling Eli raised me to my feet with her hand. "Life is precious, worlds containing the ingredients of life are crucial for humanity's survival." I heard her speak but did not see her lips move.

The blackness edged closer, I could see nothing on the other side of it. Dylan moved to speak: "We had tried to give this moon new life, but our work was not enough. We were not enough. We brought the Pegasus crew to us, and it still was not enough. We then used you to bring the Odyssey crew to us but it still was not enough."

My reality was disappearing over the edge of the nearing cliff – images of our unpacking, final transmission to Odyssey and then an unscheduled night-time trek to one of the moon's sink hole caves flashed through my mind. Eli and the others were swallowed up by an explosion of colours. Somehow, I had turned back, escaping to the surface only to run out of oxygen.

"It still was not enough." The words reverberated around the room as I realised that Morpheus had never left the Herculis system, that somehow all I had experienced had been fabricated so that the whole crew could feed organic material into whatever was residing in the caves below. My consciousness and who knows what else was plugged into Morpheus systems the whole time I had been brought back by Odyssey.

I was almost at the edge of the cliff. One after another, Eli, Dylan and Kyrsten simply dropped from my view, disappearing over the side into blackness. They had made no move and showed no surprise. They simply...went.

I had inadvertently done my job, allowing whatever I brought back with me into the systems of the ship. Crazily I found myself thinking about Morpheus; a large mothercraft full of organic material needed to sustain an extended deep space mission. Morpheus, a craft possibly large enough to provide the raw materials to bring the moon to life. Morpheus, a craft that found itself screaming through the Herculis 2 atmosphere to break her back in a plunge into a multicoloured crater lake.

FAMILY SQUABBLES

(Above) A combat craft piloted by Zarkhad hovers in high-orbit around Mars. The planet's fragile biosphere and most of its once bourgening civilisation were already in ruins. Over time, the rust-red desert sands would bury most evidence of human society from view.

Phrane was stumped. He had bad news to tell her research sponsor and was struggling to find the best way to tell him. She eventually tried honesty. "I'm sorry we don't yet have a conclusive answer as to how the interstellar war actually started."

Pokalat the sponsor, wanting to announce a major discovery to his board members, was incredulous. "How can you not know? You've spent months flitting about the galaxy and visited more archeological sites than I can count. How can you not know?"

Freya, seeing that on this occasion honesty was not the best policy, jumped in to save her colleague. "The Terran and Martian research teams also concur with this assessment. No one has yet found evidence of major uprisings, military build ups or other record. It is as if a switch was pulled and pre-history went from peace to war."

Pokalat remained unimpressed. "What sort of assessment is that? No one will believe that the interstellar war that wiped out three major civilisations in a few short years left no record?"

Phrane regained some confidence. "We have found quite a lot, actually. We know of the weaponry developed that could obliterate the entire surfaces of planets. The high radioactivity and lack of topography at Mortem is a result of the use of such weapons, not to mention Mars losing most of its atmosphere around the same time."

"So how does Mars, being much closer to Earth than Mortem, fit into this wonderful theory of yours? Surely Mars would have sided with the nearer world of Terra?"

"We have found some evidence of a visitation of a ship of Mortem origin to Mars. We think this triggered a sympathetic cause to the Martian government, putting them at odds with Earth."

Freya swooped for the knockout blow. "What's more, Laura's pyramid team have just found two bodies identified as twins. Despite lying beside each other, the military insignias they were wearing were totally different."

Pokalat was still not impressed. "So why do you think that should matter to my paying stakeholders?"

"We have identified the uniforms as belonging to high ranking officers on opposing sides of the war."

Pokalat remained confused, and Freya drove it home for him. "To summarise, we have found two officers belonging to opposing sides in the war, one of which was probably responsible for nearly destroying Mars, and they are lying next to each other in caskets we think were meant to preserve life until peace returned. This is their story."

Dawn

A small army of figures slowly walked across the horizon towards a large complex.
The morning sun rose behind them, revealing distant mountain peaks and the drying landscape of the planet Mars. The last remnant of the Free Martian defenders had to protect this barren land, once full of life, but now on the brink of total destruction.

Once they entered the building, the tired soldiers ate their breakfast meal in silence, for the war would end shortly and not in the way they had hoped for.

Despite scoring many victories for their small planet, the defenders were simply overwhelmed by the sheer weight of the enemy attacks. Mars's population was now virtually non-existent. What survivors were left was mainly due to most of the invading forces pulling out, leaving Mars's shattered environment to eat itself. A cold, empty death awaited those still alive.

The only people left to fight were currently in the Mess Hall of Zone 9; all except one man - their team leader.

Remembering

Shadom sat on his Terrain Traverser and adjusted his breathing mask. The Martian air used to be more than enough to support a diversity of wildlife, until attacks tailored to exploit the fragility of Mars caused vital oxygen to become locked into rocks and soil, leaving nothing to support life.

As light began to fill the planet's skies once more, Shadom cast his mind to happier times. Times when this silent valley was filled with the happy sounds of life and the laughter of his brother as they grew up together. Shadom could still see the outline of what was once a cool stream, a waterway he and his brother would often cool in after playing in the warm Martian sun.

(Above) Zarkhad's interceptor is shot down by the Zone 9 defenders. He struggles to right the stricken craft for a crash landing in the Martian desert. The flight performance of the interceptors flown by Zarkhad's crew was quite poor in the rapidly thinning Martian atmosphere.

His fondest memories revolved around flying. Born natural pilots, they had criss-crossed the skies in their sleek craft so many times that their airframes were simply physical extensions of themselves.

Shadom's thoughts wandered further until he reached the start of the great war between the Terran-born people and the Colonists. His brother used to sympathise with the Terran cause, disowning his Martian heritage and joining the Earth's armed forces. Shadom winced at the memory. The images returned to his head: the empty playground, the first attack and the sounds of the screams. The screams gave him nightmares each time he shut his eyes.

In an effort to forget about the dark past, Shadom rose to meet the pressures of the present day. He had only wanted one last look at his old haven for happier times, for he knew that in all likelihood, his charred body would be lying next to his memories before night claimed the valley.

Shadom's Terrain Traverser scouted around the perimeter defences. The only major form of defence left on Mars were the dubbed screamers and the huge multi-barrelled anti-aircraft weaponry. Each unit contained four black barrels that would defend Zone 9 until they too fell into the reddening dust. Then, it would all be over in a matter of seconds.

As Shadom began his trip back south, he gazed absently to some low hills. Underneath the surface were bunkers containing thousands of Martian citizens, soon to be transferred to five security pyramids made of the strongest material ever built. There, they would be put into a deep to sleep until Mars could become green once again. The protection of Zone 9 was more about buying time for the transfer to be complete. He had no illusions about the final outcome of the impending battle.

Shadom was slightly optimistic after seeing that the bulk of the enemy was pulling out. He hoped this meant that they had lost interest in Mars and the secret constructions would be left undisturbed. Arriving at headquarters, Shadom passed through heavily armoured entrance doors. As he did, he checked his personal weaponry. A twin barrelled pulse rifle. Check. Sidearm pistol. Check. And two bullets that sat in his chest pocket, one for him and the other for his brother. They had been there since the start of the war. Shadom had a premonition that one of them would be gone before he died. Which one though, which brother would die first?

Mid-Morning

A stream of harsh light broke through the window and danced through the cockpit, illuminating a face that was the shaven counterpart of Shadom. Zarkhad squinted. His hard eyes focused with an effort at the thin crescent of Mars and the filtered sun that had finally passed from behind the planet. At roughly the same time as his twin brother, he too had remembered images of happier times spent on the planet below. Passing over the site of his youth, the damage done by his invading fleet was revealed in stark view.

Bracing himself, Zarkhad took hold of the controls for his strike craft and prepared for the final attack on Mars. The battle had been clearly won by his Terran forces. As such, he ordered them to more important tasks, leaving himself and his wingman to remove the last of the Martian resistance. Then, he planned to move on and leave his childhood home forever.

Zarkhad knew that his brother was down there waiting for him, so he had left the task of annihilating his twin to himself and his trusted wing. He owed him that much. The elite First Wing slipped through the thin atmosphere as a cockpit chronometer alarm sounded. It was time to start the final assault.

Alarm

Zone 9 was in a flurry of controlled panic; a proximity klaxon rang their last warning for the members already starting to man their posts. Various detectors monitored the two Terran attack craft's approach. Their advance was shown for all to see on numerous display screens situated around the area.

Shadom relayed his orders while screamers and other defence equipment were hastily brought online. Shadom ached for an aircraft to fly, though he knew full well that he had ejected from the last Martian fighter. His little air force had accounted for themselves well, slowing the Terran onslaught until overwhelmed. Now the last of Martian air power lay smouldering on the rim of a distant crater. He and his command were strictly grounded, about to fall back on their last line of defence.

Approach

Four sets of razor-sharp wings sliced through the sky like swords of old. The planes gracefully glided through the air, Zarkhad and his wingmen believed that there was no rush to attack. Their heavily armed ships had nearly twice the ordinance necessary to vaporize Zone 9 - at least in theory. In battle there was always that small chance that things might not go the way of the attackers. For now, Zarkhad mentally inhaled the experience of flying once again in Martian skies.

He looked left and almost saw Shadom flying with him. Then his military mind kicked in and the image was replaced with the pilot of another Terran craft. Zarkhad internally kicked himself. He could no longer afford to think like that, or their mission might turn brutally sour. Weaponry was activated and the sleek crafts transformed into delivers of death.

Screamers opened fire as Zarkhad's wing came in low to the ground. The heavy rhythmic thumping accompanied with bursts of smaller fire played as everything in Zone 9's arsenal lit up. The Terran formation let loose a series of air to ground missiles, raining heavily on the base. This would be one of the last rainfalls the defenders of Mars would ever see again.

The attackers dispersed, making them harder to get hit by the screamers. Zarkhad whipped around and charged in; his craft running the gauntlet of ground to air fire. Anti-penetration shields began to strain with the number of impacts. But he had already reached his primary target: a screamer. The hapless target vanished in a blinding flash as Zarkhad's weaponry hit its mark. Another bright explosion caught Zarkhad's peripheral vision as his wingman claimed another screamer. But Zone 9 had torn one of his command out of the sky.

The screams were back. Shadom could hear them as he rushed throughout his command, helping evacuate casualties and focusing counter-attacks. As he pulled a shattered body out its burning shelter, he quickly took note of how many weapons were left. There were now only two manned screamers left to three Terran attackers. The base's defence shields were strained to limit and were on the verge of collapsing altogether.

Zarkhad exulted inwardly as he sensed the critical weakening of Zone 9's shields. He saw his command's ordinance regularly strike deep into solid buildings instead of dispersing harmlessly above. A light disappeared from his friendly fleet screen. Another member of his First Wing had 'personally' removed a screamer by piloting his burning craft into it. One left.

Shadom knew Zone 9 was finished. Most of his now vulnerable outposts were reduced to smoking hulls under Zarkhad's merciless rain. The last Martian screamer had stopped firing as its human occupant perished under a metal rain. Coldly, Shadom realised that he, two officers and three wounded sharing his traverser, were the last representatives of the Martian defence. Then he kicked the vehicle into a high-speed dash as two Terran craft banked round and came straight for him.

Weapons were locked onto the helpless fleeing traverser. Zarkhad was frustrated as the tiny vehicle was managing to dodge most of their attacks by hiding in and out of cover. Moments later, it was out in the open for a second too long. Zarkhad fired his last air to ground missile.

Incoming

Shadom's eyes widened as he saw the missile shrieking at his vehicle. Desperately he skidded right in order to avoid it. His body hammered into his seat as an explosion lifted his vehicle into the air. They landed with a deafening crash and rolled violently into some debris. No sooner had the vehicle come to rest on its back, Shadom felt an irresistible force pulling him out as two officers manhandled him to safety. Unsteadily getting to his feet, Shadom tried to turn back to look for survivors before he once more pulled back. Moments later, the vehicle and anyone left in it disappeared under a rain of strafing fire.

The remaining men looked madly for cover, for a weapon, for something that would increase their chance of survival. Even though the two craft were screaming away, they would return again and again until all three of them were dead. Suddenly Shadom's saw a chance. A screamer, control cabin smashed in, but weaponry intact, was only resting a few dozen meters from his position.

Shadom explained more in gestures than in words of his plan to the officers. In the last few seconds before Zarkhad's wing came around for another strafing run, the commander sprinted to the screamer, vaulting into its seat. He was ready.

Strike

Zarkhad exhaled; only three exposed people remained between him and Mars. With his missiles depleted, he would have to make an extreme low altitude pass to target them with his remaining weapon before they had a chance to dive for cover.

Without warning, two officers broke cover and furiously opened fire, revealing their position. Zarkhad felt sorry for them; he had seen many suicidal acts like this. He prepared fire and realised he was missing one.

Where was the third person? The screamer! The thought exploded in his head as Zarkhad suddenly noticed the screamer turning towards his wing man and realised too late that the officers' attack was a diversion.

The two attackers had allowed themselves to be ridiculously close to get in their clear shot. Shadom's screamer opened up in a booming staccato as it sent dozens of rounds shooting into Zarkhad's wingman, the closest craft.

As pieces of his wingman fell from the sky, Zarkhad's began taking evasive maneuvers. His lone craft tried to avoid the poisonous silver snake that twisted ever closer. Zarkhad tried to double back on himself, but his brother was using the screamer to anticipate his maneuvers. A series of ringing vibrations announced the armour piercing screamer rounds fatally crippling his machine.

Shadom kept firing until his target was too low for the screamer. A sudden silence fell over the battlefield. He would not declare victory just yet. He would need to confirm his kill; dividing the last of his forces on a risky undertaking. It would also mean leaving his screamer, losing control of Mars' last air defence asset. With Zone 9's control centre gone, Shadom could not know what, if any, other Terran attackers could be lying in wait out of orbit.

Orange flames surrounded Zarkhad, the heat slowly overwhelming his fire-resistant suit, burning his skin. Piloting a fatally damaged and burning striker was difficult, and the dunes and boulders of the red planet were approaching quicker that he would have liked. His helmet smashed into the cockpit controls as the stricken ship slammed into the ground, ploughing its way to an unceremonious stop.

Explosive charges threw the canopy into the air and Zarkhad half climbed out, half fell out of his seat. The crash had depleted his consumables; he was now on emergency oxygen. The last attacker on Mars hoped there would be enough for him to finish his mission.

A jet assistant unit recovered from his wrecked ship sent Zarkhad flying low over the hills to meet his brother one last time.

Sniper

Zarkhad began to feel the tiredness and fright as he set up his personal weapon on a rocky outcrop. His position allowed him to oversee the base while remaining hidden. A magnified image of a screamer briefly filled his vision as he used the rifle's scope to scan the area. Zarkhad pulled back and the focused once more onto the screamer, onto Shadom. He noted that his brother refused to give up his base's last defence, desperately scanning the area of Zarkhad's wreck. It seemed obvious that he was searching in the wrong direction.

Zarkhad panned right and identified the two other officers who had created the diversion. They were cautiously making their way to Shadom, probably not believing their plan had worked. Zarkhad turned back to Shadom and flicked a catch that armed his rocket launcher.

It was locked dead upon Shadom's chest. His hand tightened on the trigger.

A small explosion over his left shoulder caught Zarkhad's attention. One of the officers had spotted him and fired a hastily aimed round near where he lay.

A sudden reflection betrayed the presence of a binocular viewer in one of the officer's hand. He must have been scanning the horizon and accidently picked up Zarkhad. Without thinking, he acquired the new target; the weapon locked on and an anti-personnel rocket flew to greet the officer with a single-minded determination. He disappeared under a high-powered explosion; the second officer was caught mid sprint and sent cartwheeling through the blood thick air.

Shadom jumped from his screamer even as the second officer's body landed in a pitiful heap. He didn't even bother looking back to see a thin white stream of vapour rapidly fly to his screamer. He fired wildly from his own personal weapon in Zarkhad's direction. Zarkhad rewarded Shadom's efforts with a rain of high velocity fire.

Shadom crashed through some debris and tried desperately to find a safe spot to counter attack. He imagined Zarkhad coming down the ridge now, hopefully not knowing exactly where Shadom was. A shot rang out over his head. Another ricocheted off a buckled plate beside his arm, Shadom ducked and weaved trying to evade all bullets that were hunting down once more.

Finally, a thin whisper of a rocket sounded on his right and Shadom leapt to nowhere in particular. However, he kept going higher and higher. Dust, rocks and metal went with him.

Death

Slowly the smoke began to clear, allowing Zarkhad to peer from his hiding place to see if his rocket had hit its mark. He had seen Shadom fly through the air, but the ensuing debris cloud had hid him from sight. Becoming increasing frustrated with the chase; Zarkhad armed his last rocket and crept closer to where he thought Shadom had landed.

As he journeyed through the debris, Zarkhad first noticed what was left of Shadom's weapon, lying twisted on the ground in front of him. A shattered helmet visor rested nearby, most likely belonging to his brother. Stooping to picked it up, a broken reflection appeared on the shiny surface.

Zarkhad froze in realisation and slowly turned to face a bloody tower clutching a high velocity pistol. The first shot broke Zarkhads weapon in half. The second destroyed his jet pack. The third smashed his helmet visor, covering his face in millions of tiny shards. The acrid smell of a dying Mars flooded Zarkhad's senses, through his still oxygen-filled helmet. Even though his hardened suit had stopped the round from vaporizing him, Zarkhad knew that the next shot would be fatal.

Life

Shadom brought the pistol within centimetres of his twin brother's exposed face. He looked straight into the eyes that were as his own, staring at death. His grip tightened. They were finally together and all it would take to end the whole struggle for Mars was one bullet.

A bright column of light suddenly illuminated the confines of Zarkhad and Shadom's position. The Martian sun was setting, temporarily returning blue hues to a normally salmon pink sky. A breeze whipped across both men's feet; the dust twinkled in the sunlight.

"We grew up here together, Zarkhad," Shadom whispered softly. Then, he raised the pistol and sent his chambered round flying into the air. The pistol dropped. The debris around them caught myriads of reflections as the brothers swiftly changed places. After the short but violent scuffle, Shadom found himself looking down at the barrel of his own pistol. It was now in the hands of his own kin.

"In the name of the Terran Federation, I sentence you to immediate execution for your crimes against humanity." Zarkhad's eyes were set hard.

Shadom didn't move, he wasn't going to run, it was going to end here, "Why, Zarkhad?"

"It is my duty. This is why I returned to Mars. I represent the Terran defence and I will finish my mission!"

"Your mission is finished Zarkhad!" Shadom retorted with rising anger.

"Take a look around you! The last of my command lies smouldering nearby in this last zone of resistance. You've won!"

Zarkhad knew that Shadom was right. Already the thinning atmosphere was almost impossible to breathe. It would only be a matter of weeks before all standing liquid water on the Red Planet would vanish, along with the remains of the biosphere. Nevertheless, the last Martian military member, his enemy, remained before him.

"Shadom, I have to finish it. I have orders." A violent, bloody cough escaped Zarkhad's mouth. Shadom realised his twin brother was fatally wounded, condemned to die on this planet.

"Zarkhad! You're dying with the very world your leaders ordered you to destroy. Do we really want to spend our last moments together as enemies? Just look at where we are! We grew up here. We were brothers, Zarkhad…"

Zarkhad could not help but have past images of green rolling hills and swaying trees fill his thoughts. Then he saw native scenes: not armoured killers used to wipe out Zone 9, but colourful birds wheeling about in a deep turquoise Martian sky.

With an effort, he returned to the present, to Shadom. The silence was deafening. No playful chatter or gurgling water, just burning. The burning of his childhood home. Zarkhad then realised that the decades of separation and military indoctrination was not enough to break the link that the two twin brothers shared.

"Shadom, I-" … The pistol dropped to the ground as Zarkhad slumped forward, physically and emotionally spent.

Freya's research using historic records indicated the two military leaders were only together on the surface for a short time. Direct forensic analysis revealed Zarkhad's wounds would have been fatal without direct medical attention. This forced his brother to rapidly convey him to one of the Pyramids in an effort to preserve his life. With no ability to leave the dying planet, Shadom followed his twin in joining thousands of Martians already in deep sleep.

Freya, rejoining Laura's team, also found additional rooms within the security pyramids containing hundreds of caskets empty of occupants. This suggested that by the conclusion of the battle for Mars, there were not enough people left alive to fill the tiny rescue effort provided to them.

THE FINAL BATTLE

(Above) Blue 3, sole defender of Mortem, is framed by the remains of the Terran Hellfire cruiser. The destruction of the Terran cruiser was too late to save Mortem and its inhabitants.

Phrane was temporarily spared critical funding cuts from Pokalat. The price both he and Freya had to pay was to present their findings to Pokalat's stakeholder board. Rumours of planned attendance of political representatives at the meeting also added to the pressure.

"For all its devastation, the war started and ended quite quickly. It was already in its closing stages at the time of the final battle between Zarkhad and Shadom," Phrane began. "The antagonist's presence in Terran space was virtually non-existent as they had all been forced back to their home world of Mortem."

Discretely observing a Terran government representative in the audience, Freya presented her findings. "In a last desperate attempt to stop the inevitable defeat, Mortem fired hyper kinetic missiles directly at Earth and its neighbours. They entered the Terran Solar System at near-light speed, outpacing detection and defence systems."

Pokalat interrupted. "Where is the evidence for these grand assessments?"

Several stakeholders nodded in agreement. Tough crowd, Freya thought.

"What Phrane and I have found is that the missiles used on Earth were so devastating they shattered the crust near each impact site and simply wiped out much of civilisation there and then. Even after the damage caused by the impacts, the subsequent major climate changes brought about the collision were enough to erase all living memory and most records of the event. Other areas of the Solar System, and even nearby extra-solar worlds, such as near Proxima Centauri, also show evidence of non-natural surface bombardment."

"Records of the attack on Mortem and Irs are a little better than what we have for Earth, but not much. We know a single Terran 'Hellfire' cruiser made it to Mortem while its home planet was virtually wiped out. We also know a small counterattack mission was launched just before Mortem's complete destruction."

Deep in space, the last representative of Earth's vengeance closed in on Mortem. Their order was simple: "erase the civilisations of both Mortem and Irs from all living memory". The Hellfire Cruiser was aptly named for this destruction. It had evaded Mortem's planetary defence long enough to commence its firing mission.

"Target acquisition data transmitted. Prepare for immediate launch, Blue Wing. Good luck."

The message crackled through the three inter-atmosphere strike planes - all poised for launch. For a moment, all was silent before three separate engines roared to life, erupting in red and orange flames. The sleek planes slowly made their way upward as the strap-on boosters threw them off the ground. Sunlight crept into the three cockpits as the strikers soared out of their underground resting place.

Condensation briefly shrouded the crafts as they broke the sound barrier in their rapid climb to the heavens. They tore through the smog layer and rose above the clouds in their journey through the sky. One pilot disengaged her attention from her instruments and looked out into the distant horizon. A slim building spire rose above the smog, greeting the Blue Flight wing commander. It marked the location of the Colonist Empire's greatest city. Blue 1 thought it was almost shameful to see the once proud and defiant superpower of this region reduced to a dying planet. The burning world was the home of those descendants of human beings exiled centuries ago in the Exodus. And all this began with the foolish attempt of some of their number trying to return home. That action had led to this bitter war – the bloodiest conflict humanity had ever seen.

Suddenly, her attention was caught by what looked like a fiery comet penetrating the upper atmosphere. It was streaking down in a perfect arc before disappearing with a blinding flash of light.

Another hellfire cruiser missile had found its target. They had started raining down on the planet for the last two days and despite the best efforts of ground defences, had succeeded in vaporising ninety percent of Mortem's surface.

Blue Wing silently mourned the loss of lives and their once beautiful planet. As they passed the fringes of the outer atmosphere, it was no longer possible to distinguish Mortem's geography. Mountains, valleys, rivers, and other familiar features were hidden under the pervasive smog layer caused by the missile attack. Cut off from their home world a quiet transmission was simultaneously received and heard by all three transceivers.

"Base to Blue Team…I…I don't know how to put this to you, but we may no longer be here on your return. All of us down here give you our best hopes, to whatever future you might have left."

"Blue 1 to base, understood and thank you." As Blue 1 ended the transmission, she felt a wave of sadness wash over her. None of the wing was surprised. An assessment of the damage-rate prior to their launch had estimated complete saturation of Mortem's surface from missile attacks before the

(Above) The Terran system prior to the bombardment of the interstellar war. Earth's Moon was terraformed, just like early Mars. It's fragile biosphere stood no chance against the hyperkenetic attacks. The Moon shielded Earth from some of the destruction, at the expense of being completely sterilized.

Blue team could complete their mission.

"Blue Wing, this is Blue 1. You have just heard the message from the ground. I am sorry for all of us but now we need to stay on task and complete our mission." As the other two wing members called in their acknowledgement, Blue 1 thought it best to let them quickly have their own thoughts and get on with what needed to be done.

In her cockpit, Blue 3 also pondered the goodbye message. She was the youngest in terms of combat experience, having only flown limited and low-risk security missions. Although she had followed current events along with all her colleagues, the transition of her home world from a green paradise to ashes left her spiralling. Her sorrow had quickly given way to anger. She was angry at the Terran military force, at the Earth government, at the entire universe for allowing this to happen.

With a struggle Blue 3 pushed those feelings to the background and focused on her flight. She accepted the goodbye message with cold resolve like her two other companions.

Blue 1 felt a slight jolt as her craft, along with the others, shed the launch boosters and entered an arcing trajectory that would take them behind Mortem's moon to their target. By now they were travelling at a terrific speed, rapidly eating up the distance between themselves and the enemy cruiser. They would shortly be within weapons range.

A notification alarm briefly beeper sounded in Blue 1's cockpit, accompanied by 'NETCOM LOST' message that flashed on her transceiver display. The fighter had just lost contact with their base back on Mortem, which up until then was linking the wing commander's craft with a fragile lifeline of data. They were quite close to the cruiser now, perhaps the enemy had jammed the communications link. Radiation from the missile attacks had probably wrecked the ionosphere, playing havoc with communications, or…

Thousands of perfectly logical reasons invaded her mind as she tried to divert her thinking from the most likely possibility: the base might no longer exist.

Blue 1 acted quickly, before her command could ask awkward questions and especially before her panic could kick in and make her lose complete control of current situation. She had to focus on the current mission ahead and there was time to worry about the base.

Blue 1: "All craft switch to combat configuration and confirm battle readiness!"

Blue 2: "Blue 2 confirm."

Blue 3: "Blue 3 confirm."

Almost simultaneously Blue Wing switched their weaponry from 'SAFE' to 'ARM' and gave their fire control systems authority to target. The three craft used the gravity of Mortem's moon to swing around and face the ominous large shape in front of them. Narrow angle feeds showed the enemy hellfire cruiser had both of its weapon bay doors open, releasing another missile to make its way to Mortem. Blue 1's tracking system was also able to monitor the missiles' flight all the way back to Mortem where it annihilated yet another hapless target.

As the strikers prepared to attack, it became obvious that the cruiser was unaware of their presence, for now at least. The fire control system in Blue 1's cockpit lit up – it was able to prosecute its target. Blue 1 knew it was time to take their revenge.

"I'm taking the target," she announced, "Attack configuration!" Her craft thrusted forward, away from her group and two seconds later, long cylindrical missiles detached from the underside of her craft and sped away.

"First one and first two away!"

The other two craft maneuvered into their combat trajectories. Blue 2 fired a long-range missile with the call of "First 3!"

The missiles soared towards the carrier. All three pilots sighed thankfully as their weapons hit their mark. The body of the cruiser shuddered violently as the force of the detonations shoved it sideways. Blue 1's congratulatory message was interrupted by a weapons threat alarm in her headset. The cruiser's crew had finally detected their attackers and sensors were rapidly locking onto the three small strikers. Almost immediately afterward, the region around Blue Wing was filled with bursts of light and energy as the cruiser retaliated with a variety of military systems.

Blue 1, being the first to attack, was the closet to the barrage. She saw the great danger. "Evasive maneuvers!" she screamed her last orders while dumping her remaining ordnance into the cruiser and executing an emergency retro thrust burn.

Blue 2 put up a barrage of supporting fire to buy his leader time, but it was too late. Blue 1 pushed her craft so hard that her wing thought it would break up. Then she was hit. Then again. And again. An energy beam cut Blue 1 in half, but the cruiser kept firing until the stricken attacker vanished from their view.

The remaining Blue team scattered before they shared the same fate as their commander. There was no time to mourn the loss of the one who, like family, had shepherded them until now. She had tried to reassure them that the Terran forces would feel the wrath of Mortem's last defenders, but she had been wrong.

The remaining Blue wing saw the cruiser closing its missile bays and preparing for departure. The Terran ship had been hit quite badly and probably did not wish to stay near an already doomed Mortem.

Blue 2 observed the cruiser's trajectory burns, and suddenly surmised its next destination. One more viable world in this system remained. Currently desolate, Irs would, over time, become a second Mortem. Hundreds of machines and the thousands of colonists were mining volatiles, spewing gasses into the sky for the planet Irs to become a abode of life.

Irs would be a far easier target than Mortem, with military defence virtually non-existent. Fearing Irs would share the same fate as Mortem, what was left of Blue Wing decided they could not allow the cruiser to leave.

As the dark behemoth fired its powerful engines to pull itself out of orbit, Blue 2 screamed in, strafing its flank. Blue 3 moved in from behind and lay down withering fire. Numerous craters and minor explosions erupted on the dark hull careening below them as their weaponry found its mark. Dumping much of their fuel, the small strikers arced around for another pass – to be met with lethal defensive fire.

Then Blue 2 was gone. Changing attitude for a targeting solution, he had somehow found himself at the cruiser's front. Expenditure of all his remaining missiles and short range ordnance failed to prevent energy burst cutting through his cockpit and into the main engines, vaporising his craft.

Blue 3 passed over the cruiser and kept going. Accelerating away, she could not admit to herself that she was running away, trying to evade battle. Away from the vivid sight of seeing her two friends fall apart before her own eyes, away from the cruiser, away from death. Caught in a high orbit arc from Mortem's moon, she was surprised to see Irs rise above the cratered landscape. Little more than a star at this distance, Blue 3 saw the final location of all that remained of her kind.

Blue 3 throttled down her engines. She realised there was nowhere to go in her short range ship. The fate of thousands of people depended on what she would do next. The last of Blue Wing modified her trajectory to follow a tight orbit around Mortem's moon. The cratered surface below her zoomed by, with mountain peaks missing her craft by mere metres. Soon the ground became more distant as her orbit took her back into outer space.

Eventually the hellfire cruiser rose above the moon's crescent and Blue 3 saw that it was preparing to jump out of the Mortem system. A shimmering aura surrounded the cruiser and increased in intensity as an extra-dimensional door started to open between it and the next target, Irs.

"First four," Blue 3 said to herself as she launched her long-range missiles. The last weapons of the Colonists sped away and hit the cruiser's amidships, seconds later. The aura collapsed on itself and bright colours flooded Blue 3's cockpit.

Her eyes sparkled at the wonderful sight as the collapsing warp field cycled through the visible spectrum, gradually dissipating energy into the disintegrating cruiser. Then her spirits broke when she thought of the people who had just died, both on board the cruiser and on Mortem. She no longer even had her fellow pilots for company.

The last of the beautiful colours faded away as the radiation of the field's collapse shifted below the spectrum visible to the human eye. The ochre globe of Mortem and its moon below were Blue 3's only companions. With the action of the battle gone as well, the young woman realized her complete isolation for the first time. Her fingers absently traced the outline of the transceiver display. The screens were blank, the intelligence feed to base long gone and green markers of her colleagues now absent. Not even the blinking of the enemy cruiser's position was present.

Turning her gaze to deep space, she assessed the two options before her. Although she wished she could travel to Irs, her craft was only designed as short-range fighter. The attack had burned so much fuel that Blue 3 couldn't go much further than the distance she had already travelled. She could stay where she was, sending a message to Irs and hoping that someone could rescue her. This was not likely as Blue 3 would have long suffocated by the time anything made the journey. That was assuming they would receive a low power message sent on a tactical military system anyway.

Blue 3 could instead return to Mortem. A graveyard. She hoped there was a slim chance someone else survived on the planet. They could be hidden in some deep recess underground, unable to call out, but nonetheless alive.

She knew the return trip would to be one-way. After atmospheric entry, descent and landing there would be no fuel to take off again. Taking a sharp breath in, Blue 3 made her decision. She turned her craft around and executed a high power burn to break out of orbit.

Activating the landing sequence, the small ship soon smashed into Mortem's murky atmosphere. The ride was bumpy as searing winds and turbulence forced her to jettison most of her ship and continue in the more stable lander section. An alarm sounded and Blue 3 noticed the radiation sensor on her environment monitor was going off the scale. She was shocked to discover the whole planet, including the atmosphere was fiercely radioactive. It would only be a matter of hours before the Terran-made fallout penetrated her cockpit, subjecting Blue 3 to a lethal radiation dose.

She flew lower, calling through the transceiver and simultaneously trying to pick up a stray signal that might have indicated the presence of other survivors. Only the random cracks and pops of radiation greeted her transmissions.

The craft broke through the lower smog layer, revealing the ground below. Blue 3 was shocked at what she saw, or more of what she didn't. The extent of destruction was worse than she imagined. Her flight path was supposed to take her over a snow-capped mountain range, but it was now a mere flat pockmarked expanse.

Flying in the direction of her base, Blue 3 tried desperately to find a familiar landmark. There was nothing. She began to lose focus, not quite appreciating what she was seeing. Her whole body felt numb. Like everyone else here, she once had a family on Mortem, people she cared about.

Blue 3 only took a couple more minutes to reach the location of her base. Neither her eyes, nor her cockpit sensors could find any trace of the former Colonist stronghold amidst the glazed rubble strewn across the surface. As Blue 3 landed, the reality that she was the only person left alive on this dead planet sunk in. Without a moment's hesitation, she threw her cockpit canopy open and climbed out. Radiation monitors screamed in virtual agony as she did so. Only minutes remained before Blue 3's fragile life would be extinguished by the legacy of the Terran attack.

The soft crunch of her boots as they touched the glassy regolith were the only sounds she could hear. Walking absently, Blue 3 stooped to pick up a small fragment from the ground. She turned it over in a morbid curiosity, wondering which part of her base it used to be. Then she threw it away as far as she could.

In a last gesture of despair, the lone woman tore off her flight helmet, exposing her bare face to the environment. She sank to her knees and sobbed into her gloved hands. Her tears dried quickly in the desiccating heat. Mortem's air, once gentle and cool but now seared with dry heat and sterilising radiation, dispersed the cries of the planet's last inhabitant.

Thousands of years of exposure to high temperatures and ionising radiation failed to prevent the discovery of Blue 3's craft by Phrane's joint survey team. Partially buried in the desiccant soil, the rotten hulk, merely a shadow of the proud craft it had once been, retained an air of dignity. It was the final outpost, the last representative of a sad struggle that had destroyed over 12 billion lives.

The war had concluded with no clear winners. The once proud Terran home world was stilled to a loud silence, as the survivors of the Great War were faced with the hardship of rebuilding their society. It would be many centuries before Earthlings could once again leave their home planet and explore the cosmos. This time proved too long for the Martians. Their deep sleep within the pyramids transitioned to the eternal sleep of death as life support machinery failed.

Centuries would also pass before the Narriwa finished their long task of making Irs livable. The immediate focus of maintaining critical systems and staying alive removed any thought of exploration beyond Irs for its people. Aging memories and natural attrition of time reduced the terraforming process to a distant legend.

Following their meeting with Pokalat's stakeholders, Freya and Phrane were able to generate enough government interest to have the Blue 3 artefact recovered and placed on permanent display at the Galactic Museum of History. It silently reminds future generations of the extreme price society pays for human rebellion.

The final moments of the Blue 3 pilot at the former location of where she and her colleagues had left the planet. Mortem's moon peeps through the smog-ridden and heavily radioactive sky. Mortem's toxic environment even proved fatal to many robotic probes launched by a redeveloping Irs society sent to explore the once pristine planet.

THE AWAKENING

(Above) Jordan, sole survivor of the Pyramid people, visits the memorial site of her friends. Despite her huge personal loss, Jordan has been very generous with helping the numerous researches and scholars wishing to recreate the turbulent period of her past.

The Martian ecosystem was finally restored to sustain human life and the doors of the Martian pyramids stood open. For millennia the previously sealed hallways and rooms within the pyramids stood silent. Housing undisturbed bodies of an early race for centuries was quite unbelievable; access to these pyramids triggered the largest research and archeology effort since the discovery of the much older Martian ruins of the cold, desiccated Mars of an earlier era. A truly interstellar team of Terran and Irs professionals focused their efforts on analysing what lay inside the pyramids. While not overtly stated, the joint team felt a subtle but noticeable political pressure on making astounding discoveries. The accolades of the Breen mission to symbolically reunite Earth and Irs were fading from memory, along with the participants themselves. Ongoing discoveries of the Exodus, plus the many ravaged monuments from the interstellar war were present in most recent memories, generating much commentary. In light of this political landscape, leaders of both planets were keen to demonstrate that former enemies were capable of conducting a major, peaceful undertaking.

Inside the pyramids, the interior construction and aging facilities were subjected to the minor scrutiny of a small number of dedicated researchers. The bulk of the effort and thus the most research were focused on the rows and rows of caskets containing human remains dressed in what was left of their environment suits. Up to this point the research team had consisted of forensic scientists, archeologists and environmental control experts. One particular room, the designated Room 419, the special attention of a team of professional staff never before seen inside the pyramids: paramedics.

"Hurry up doctor," a middle-aged woman called behind her as she strode purposefully through the halls of a pyramid, outpacing a man in medical attire stumbling five meters behind. The sounds of their footsteps echoed in the wide halls as they both made their way to a newly-installed tactical medical centre. The woman strode with such footed grace that it was obvious she had grown up in the reduced Martian gravity. The same couldn't be said for her companion who ran with a clumsy stride, betraying his Earth origin. He was also a fair deal shorter than her, as Martians routinely grew to heights of nearly two metres.

Laura and her earthly companion turned right into another pristine white hallway and halted at a pair of guarded automatic doors. Following an embarrassing incident where the doctor actually stumbled against the doors, the guards granted access and ushered them in.

Laura saw her team swarming around one certain casket discovered an hour previously. This particular rectangular-shaped container had one certain quality that the others lacked: it was still operational. Dozens of blue-suited people worked feverishly to rescue the solitary occupant from the aging prison. Laser cutters were brought in and sliced through a canopy that time and corrosion had sealed shut. Life resuscitators of a stabilizing unit had already been brought in and the limp figure was gingerly transferred over to an intense rescue unit. The body had no sooner come to rest in a sterilized liquid bath, when a complex assortment of tubes and devices was attached to that person' yellowish skin. Despite the procedure being the first of its kind, the medical team worked efficiently using the latest items in life support equipment.

A hitherto dormant health monitor displayed a small burst of life. The delicate process of resurrection traced its path into the dormant body as phosphorescent lines and pulses vibrated around and inside the patient's feeble body shape. Other vital statistics were beginning to be displayed whilst Laura, now supervising the medical team's efforts, noted with interest that the survivor was a female. The process of transferring the body from her casket to the stabilizing unit had only taken eleven minutes and Laura watched as her medical team rushed out quickly to secure their prize.

They were directed into an airlock where Laura and her companion proceeded to put on their isolation suits. As they underwent a decontamination procedure, Laura was surprised to see an isolation suit-clad political correspondent in the room waiting for them. "Can I have a moment, please, Laura?" the correspondent asked.

"Another off-worlder," Laura thought, noticing the correspondent's diminutive stature. She also rapidly understood the real purpose of his surprise visit: to report the success of the joint pyramid exploration mission. "Make it quick," she shot back as the Terran doctor used the distraction to quietly quit the room.

"Clearly this discovery has significant implications to our understanding of our respective culture's pre-history. Could you briefly describe how you came across this discovery?"

Laura recalled the momentous events that had just occurred inside Pyramid One. She was leading her team through cataloging the unusual occupants in their caskets - all undergoing different stages of decomposition.

"Analysis is ongoing, but we think the different states of decay in the bodies suggest the caskets were occupied over a period of time, not all at once. Our team had entered one of the latest rooms to be accessed and saw some bodies appearing to be only recently deceased."

At that time Laura thought it strange that despite the rows and rows of human remains, there was no accompanying death smell. The atmosphere inside Pyramid One was unnaturally sterile, unnerving the team. "We were progressing to the back of the room, moving slowly due to the presence of ancient equipment blocking our passage – then my team found the operational casket." Laura also remembered the shouts of both shock and excitement echoing through the walls and making their way into her ears. Laura recalled her heart pounding and the feelings that nearly overcame her as to what her discovery would mean for humanity.

The correspondent was about to ask Laura another question when a small alarm chimed on her bracelet.

"Excuse me," she said while bounding to the intensive care unit, too fast for the stumbling off-worlder to follow.

"She's not fully awake yet," the Terran doctor whispered on seeing Laura's arrival. She noticed the doctor was hardly moving as if unconsciously implying that any sudden motion could distress the already unconscious survivor. "Her brain activity is increasing rapidly though, and we expect her to be fully conscious within minutes." The doctor followed turning to open the airlock before saying to Laura: "You're going to be the first person she's seen since the time she was put into that pyramid. So, it's probably best that you are female." Then without further words, he opened the airlock and stepped back to allow Laura to pass through. The room was completely silent apart from Laura's faint steps as she carefully approached the stabilizer.

The enclosure was dominated by a mass of medical equipment nearly concealing a tiny figure floating in the tank of clear liquid. Laura paused, preparing herself for what she was about to see. She could make out the woman more clearly now, as she approached once more. Her figure appeared almost completely wasted away making her look like a skeleton enveloped in a yellowish skin layer laced through with bright, blue veins, rather than a living person. Her closed eyes were shrunken inside their expressionless sockets.

Laura looked from outside the tank and held her breath as she noticed that the girl's moving eyelids. The moments that immediately followed her awakening were critical; the guards had been ordered to not even admit political ministers without the express permission of Laura and the medical doctor. There were already ever-increasing number of senior scientists desperate to interview the survivor for their Martian pyramid research.

After what seemed like an hour, the girl finally fully opened her eyes. She stared blankly at the ceiling for a couple of moments until her long-disused eyes became accustomed to the input. Then, her sad gaze drifted across the room and her puzzled expression fell onto Laura's face. The two women's eyes locked and they both smiled in mutual understanding that surpassed language and time.

Much later, Laura again found herself before the political correspondent to provide what would become an almost unending series of interviews.

"The pyramids proved to be the final link that explained the chain of events that have puzzled generations of historians on both Earth and Irs," she summarized. "Their architecture and newly-discovered records contained within them are providing the key to unlock the past of the Red Planet."

Analysis of the millennia-old records and other artifacts contained within the Martian pyramids would occupy researchers for decades. In the months following the revival of Jordan – a name the survivor had picked for herself as uncultured newcomers could never pronounce her name correctly.

Laura had increasingly distanced herself from her team. Spending time with the found girl, Jordan, was her new focus. This process was not easy. Soon after the discovery of the living lady Jordan, Pokalat and his stakeholders had descended upon Laura's team. To say she was hounded by the sponsor group was an understatement; actually, Laura was almost dragged inside the unbelievably lavish office of her project underwriter, Pokalat, by his personal assistant.

"You need to understand, Laura, that these are delicate times in a political sense. The heady days of First Contact are well behind us. All involved in that mission are long dead and now society's more recent memories are occupied with the grisly discoveries your team has unearthed."

Laura bristled but remained coldly polite. "I agree, we coordinated our work under your direct specifications. In fact, as I recall, Freya and Phrane, part of the joint Mars/Irs field team, had to repeatedly report, and justify their findings to your stakeholder group."

"I appreciate that, but you must see that this has uncovered a larger issue here. Terraforming Mars was the latest major achievement and showed how independent governments could work together. However, even this achievement is overshadowed by discoveries of weapons so powerful they have wiped out entire planets. There is increasing unrest in Irs circles that are perceiving the Terran system as the antagonist in this historical conflict."

"Maybe because Terra was in some way responsible," Laura responded. "But this was thousands of years ago. Surely the success of our joint mission is showing that we can work together?"

"Not as much as you would think," Pokalat countered. "There is an extremist faction on a planet near the half-way point between Earth and Irs called 'the Scar.' They have infiltrated a disenfranchised colonist group to start a civil war. Other disparate factions are becoming more unified on Earth. To them, the distant memories of first contact and the fading memory of Mars terraforming are overshadowed by the far greater consequences of the interstellar war."

Laura was becoming suspicious. "Just what is your interest and involvement in monitoring these extremist uprisings? We are government-supported research, aren't we? Just what resources have you been using to undertake this intelligence work?"

"Please don't try to pretend that our history has nothing to do with what is happening now. You know as well as I do that senior government officials would like to see that our work ensures stability across the Alliance. I, like you, I am sure, would also like to see us do what we can to support that cause."

Laura, hiding her incredulity and not liking the way the discussion was going, wondered when her sponsor would eventually come to the point. Suddenly an ugly realization dawned on her.

"Why have you been hounding Phrane and Freya and insisting that they gather evidence about the strategies and weapons used in the interstellar war? Come to think of it, what do you know about the random disappearances of recovered artifacts from our stores? Please tell me that you haven't been using our work for military weapons development?"

Pokalat, ensuring he had built his team from the best and brightest researchers available, knew he had only himself to blame that eventually one of them would stumble on his discrete activities. "Centuries ago, the Foxhound demonstrated just how much of an advantage it is to have powerful forces in your possession. Of course we keep these hidden in the deepest of recesses, and only to be used at the darkest, most desperate hour of need. The political correspondent who interviewed you has been very helpful in our unlocking the potential of the past for keeping us safe in the future."

Laura was growing very concerned. "You know the Foxhound event, fighting for survival, does not compare with what we understand happened in the interstellar war. Surely the Alliance would need to decide what is best to do with this research, as a joint undertaking. Just how much is the Alliance in agreement with what you are doing? And what has it got to do with me?"

"Our stakeholders have built a quorum of like-minded corporate and government parties. When the time comes, we will be able to demonstrate to the Alliance just how much they will need this capability." Pokalat shifted in his seat a little. "As to your second question, I understand you have been taking good care of the Pyramid survivor, Jordan?"

It was Laura's turn to squirm in her seat. "What has Jordan got to do with your questionable research?" she snapped, already surmising the answer.

"You are intelligent enough to know that the one living link between our time and the interstellar war is in your care. We both know that she would, with assistance, provide invaluable information to help restore stability. Not only from a military standpoint but also from political and policy perspectives. We are very interested to know how the early governments manage their people in response to the threat of war?"

Laura stood up to leave, but saw that the doors to Pokalat's office were suddenly closing. The 'personal assistant' had also taken position in front of the doors, shielding them with his bulk. "Please, Jordan is still physically and psychologically fragile. She is not ready for this," she pleaded.

Pokalat shook his head in a gesture meant to be sympathetic. "That is why I will be entrusting the bulk of the work to your expertise. These facilities – yours and Jordan's new residence by the way – are fantastically well equipped and will provide you access to the latest in post-traumatic care. I am sure Jordan will be very pleased with her new home when she arrives here in a few hours."

Laura, looking absolutely defeated, slowly sat down, crossed her right hand over her left and pressed hard on her bracelet. An angry red light flashed once, bright enough for all to notice, then settled into a steady orange pulse.

"What is that?" Pokalat asked. The personal assistant did not change his position.

"Oh, just a new research experiment in anti-jammable transmissions," Laura replied. "Jordan has one just like it and it is also now activated. The Terran First Minister gave us these, realizing just how important keeping Jordan safe was to the interests of the Alliance."

Pokalat unconsciously leaned back in his chair to distance himself from the device.

"The First minister acted as part a joint agreement with the other Alliance ministers. She assured us that on the bracelets' activation, all available Alliance Security would respond at once to ensure our rescue and safety, regardless of our location. The Terran First Minister also ensured that she herself would physically be present at our location within 48 hours of signal activation," she added. "I am just researching how long it will actually take for these folk to arrive."

A week later, the fresh sea breeze and the cool morning air greeted Jordan as she stepped out onto her new balcony. Seventy floors above the Mars' surface, she was enjoying a spectacular view of her home world. It looked like a Mars before the war with Earth – an image which she remembered so well. That was before the sleep when the sky was of a similar deep blue, turquoise to be precise. Mars Terraforming project that resurrected a large portion of the old Mars ecosystem was bringing familiar scenes to her memory.

As she looked further, Jordan was able to faintly see the Martian pyramids, her previous resting place. It had taken a long time for her to adjust to her new life, but those times were finally drawing to a close.

"Jordan!" a female voice called from behind her. It was Laura.

Like Jordan, Laura was enjoying her former project sponsor's 'gift' of his former Martian offices. The events following her bracelet activation had occurred rather quickly. Pokalat's personal assistant had rushed his executive out of the office, convincing him that if he wanted to escape, he had to leave immediately. As they passed Laura, still in her chair, the assistant had given her a slight nod. It seemed that Alliance Security was a lot closer to Laura's location than even she had realised.

Quietly, Pokalat and a number of high-level personnel fell out of public view, and were never referred to again in any forum. The First Minister, arriving as promised, had thanked Laura and Jordan for their help in maintaining stability, and asked if they could help the Alliance in maintaining stability. To assist them, the First Minister offered them well-equipped offices that had just become available for new occupancy. Laura and Jordan had readily agreed.

"Jordan, are you out here?" The voice sounded closer and was followed directly by Laura herself.

(Above) Strato-jumping became the new sporting craze soon after Mars was terraformed. Jordan and Laura often watched dare devils jump from the top of Mars' atmosphere and plunge at high - and often fatal - speeds to an equally risky landing.

Jordan turned and smiled happily when she saw her old friend.

"So, what do you have planned for today?" Jordan spoke with a clear accent, a result of hard work at language study.

As Laura outlined the day's adventure, Jordan listened with great interest. She enjoyed spending time with Laura, who had always been there for her during the hard times. Those times were where she spent entire months with Jordan screaming in pain. Her struggle to familiarize herself with the present era and to make sense of her life was over and for this, she was extremely grateful to her friend.

It would have been impossible if not for Laura to get through it all. But Laura had been there to offer love, patience and medical help. Now, years after her awakening, most of the questions of the past had been answered and the healing process was complete. And all that was due in part to these small adventures she had with Laura.

Today, they were going to go further than ever into the Valles Marineris Preserve for a leisurely swim in the newly-flooded valley system's cool, deep waters.

They left for their journey in a hypersonic vacuum train that soon crossed the few thousand kilometres between Jordan's apartment and their destination. Jordan was still not quite used to seeing people walking safely along the surface of Mars, not worrying about enemy air strikes. She then remembered that the enemy, and the threat it held over Mars, was long dead.

As the two women left the station, Jordan could smell the sweet water and hear the faint calls of joy as people dived from the Valley Plunge. The Valley Plunge was a series of dive platforms that, by Terran standard, were impossibly high. In fact, diving from platforms of this height on Earth would have been fatal. Despite this, many Terrans eagerly jumped off the Valley Plunge to experience a graceful fall in Mar's lighter gravity.

Laura raced to the water as soon as it was in her view, with Jordan eagerly following after her. The blue, clear liquid enveloped her legs as she slowly made her way into its depths. Lifting her head up, Jordan could see the Mariners Motel, a multi-story rest-haven that rose up above the canyon walls. All was peaceful as she looked down at the spectacular canyon view. Suddenly, what looked like an oversized transparent bird flew dangerously close to them, causing Laura to shriek.

"Sorry about that!" The glider's pilot yelled out as he struggled to regain control of his fragile craft. A lightweight propulsion system shot the contraption away and the pilot rushed to join some other flyers who were trying to outdo each other in acrobatic maneuvers.

Jordan shook her head mockingly, "Off-world tourists! You can recognise them anywhere."

"Yes, do you recall when we went to Irs? We looked so out of place!" Laura perked up.

During their trip to Irs, they had made the pilgrimage to the memorial site where Marshal Breen and Karn Slikchovix had shaken hands in the official First Contact ceremony.

Jordan smiled inwardly, remembering the serenity she felt that moment. Poor Laura must have been so embarrassed that day. Jordan had promised herself again and again that she wasn't going to cry. However, as soon as they were near the site, she had collapsed into bawling tears in front of everyone. Mind you, they were not tears of sadness, but of joy. The memorial helped both Terran, Martians and Irs people remember that they were one race. For them, the monument signified forgiveness and stepping away from war that had left her asleep for millennia.

Laura was a bit teary herself after recalling the trip, "I'm glad no one recognised us; the trip was supposed to be a sort of counseling for you! The last thing we needed was a hundred interviewers descending on us."

As the day advanced, they continued to chat lightly about visited places and embraced the relaxation the valley offered.

Soon the weather cooled as Phobos, Mar's closest moon, approached silently. The station was quiet as most people had already left the valley by the time the moons were up on the horizon. Jordan could no longer smell the water as the train doors closed and the vehicle accelerated to a speed once reserved for space travel. The journey back home was short in duration and Laura disembarked. Jordan remained on board the train and Laura didn't ask why, as she understood her friend needed time alone.

The sun started to sink when Jordan arrived at her next destination, the Pyramids Memorial. She gripped a Martian flower and steadied herself as she crossed the fields that bore both decorative plants and graves. Every month she made her way here to attend her own memorial service. She would lay her own wreath made of flowers made to grow in the once sterile soil. The Martian wind blew at her, troubling her spirit while she thought of all the dead people whose names were engraved on the crystal crosses erected in their honour. The dead were not buried under the memorial crosses. Instead, following completion of the bulk of the forensic research, Jordan had requested they remain inside their resting place, sealed forever inside the security pyramids. Many names on the crosses were old friends, but most were complete strangers. Each person mentioned in the cemetery had some part to play in the Interstellar War – none were untouched by the conflict.

Jordan had a small role; she had been one of the victims caught in the middle of this war; she fought no battle, but instead had merely been a refugee rushed into the Pyramids where she was put to sleep to await her future, like many of the others. Yet she was the only survivor, the heroine no longer entombed.

She turned down to walk alongside another row and stopped at a particular cross. It was that of a little girl, called Clarissa, she had looked after during the short period of running towards the Pyramids. Jordan lowered her eyes as she remembered the girl's grip on her hands. How hard had Clarissa tried to return to her dead mother laying a few metres away from help.

The girl's shoes were missing. She was hardly able to walk. Jordan had picked her up and did not look back. Enemy planes were quickly gaining on them and the metal rain of their weapons was deathly close. Then, a shot from nowhere hit Jordan in the leg causing her to fall, still clutching onto Clarissa. The child had taken this moment to run back to her mother. Jordan had tried to stop her. She had been so close, a few more paces and Jordan could have grabbed her again. But it was too late. Before blacking out herself, Jordan glimpsed Clarissa being hit from the enemy strike.

Jordan always tried to visit this site; she always spoke to it as if Clarissa was her sister, her own loss.

"Laura and I had such a great time together today. Mars has these glider things now, for fun. I think Laura really wants to fly one." No word came out of the cross, it remained silent as always.

A single tear fell as Jordan put the flowers down near Clarissa's cross and rose to leave.

"Something about this is not quite right," she thought to herself, looking at the cross again. Jordan remembered something Clarissa had told her a long time ago. A simple desire of a child before the war had cut things short. Rousing herself, Jordan came to a decision.

"We have one more journey to do together," she said once more to the cross. "A friend needs our help. We need to do this last thing before we can finally say good bye."

HOSTING A MUSEUM

(Above) The hardships of surviving in alien environments caused many Exodus colonies to regress. Critical skills and technology were lost, morphing into myths and legends of a bygone past.

Several kilometres below the planet's mean elevation, several hundred people wearing blue cloaks gathered beneath an impressive construction of masonry. The structure was adorned with line artwork depicting abstract versions of space flight. Here was what looked like a helmeted figure; there was what might have been a spacecraft. The pinnacle and the focus of the construction were those of a derelict spacecraft held aloft on its rocky tower, its innards exposed to the elements.

One of the oldest of the gathering wore the brightly coloured garb of one clearly in charge. He stood underneath the wrecked craft. Standing before him, under the light of a strange moon, was a younger man, wearing the purple robe of a junior initiate.

The elder struck his staff, made of exotic metal alloy, twice on the pavement stones, officially starting the night's ceremony.

"Who are we, Junior Navigator?" he asked of the person before him, and loud enough for the rest of the group to hear.

"We are the cursed travellers, Grand Pilot. Cast from our homes," the Junior Navigator replied.

"Where have we come from?"

"From lands separated by oceans of dark space and time."

"Where are we now?"

"We are home. The home of Our Land, Our Earth, Our Ground."

The Grand Pilot smiled. His son had worked and studied for this event for years, the ceremony marking his graduation.

"Welcome Junior Navigator, to our ranks. You, like the rest of us, are charged with working Our Ground, forever turning your eyes away from the cursed sky from where we came. The cursed object atop our temple is forever consigned to our past. You and Our Ground are our future."

Then something happened that was not part of the ceremony. The Junior Navigator looked up at the same instant as a point of light appeared, rapidly brightening as it moved across the night sky. He was the only one to see the object, and could not help but watch as it passed directly overhead, slowly dimmed and disappeared as it set into the planet's shadow.

Even as the now-graduated Junior Navigator committed to a life of toil producing much-needed agricultural produce for a struggling culture, his life would never be the same.

Out of sight from his father, the Junior Navigator would secretly scan the night skies with a stolen telescope and record observations. He had searched for—and eventually found—the satellite he spotted at the ceremony, and had divined it as a small object circling his planet.

During the day, he faithfully toiled for the Grand Pilot, working like most of the community to ensure that all had enough to eat. Then he would pay his respects to the ruins of the ceremony site and, sure that no one was looking, would 'borrow' yet more artifacts to pore over in the night.

Rapidly rising through the Navigator levels and beating many of his peers to Assistant Pilot, he prepared to once again face his father to take over as Grand Pilot.

Prematurely summoned to the older man's chamber, he entered to see his father in tears, and was shocked to see the stolen telescope in his hands.

"Father, I…" the younger man stumbled.

"Say no more. I have been watching you for a long time, including your secret visits to the off-limits ceremonial site."

"But those 'relics' can help us. So far I have been able to make crops grow where there was once arid ground, Our Ground."

The soon-to-be-retired Grand Pilot nodded. "You are about to become Grand Pilot, leader of Our Land. Don't lead our people back to the cursed darkness!"

"Why do we need to hate the sky so much?" The younger man blurted out after hearing yet again the emphasis on 'land, ground, earth'.

"I came from the sky. It was My Land. Thousands of my ancestors were cursed to travel the oceans of darkness. I don't know how long they travelled, living their whole existence trapped in My Land. There were only a few hundred left when we finally reached Our Ground."

"I still don't understand."

"Perhaps you never will. We had lost nearly everything, and many more of us died trying to survive on Our Ground. We chose to forget, leaving the relics of the cursed travel behind. We instead worked hard for Our Earth to provide us what we needed to eat."

"I can use the cursed relics to help Our Land. Teach the Junior Navigators the wisdom of the sky."

The older man frowned. "No Grand Pilot will ever touch objects of the cursed sky. Turn your back on this madness and work Our Land."

Centuries later, a small craft flew through the planet's thin atmosphere. The landscape scrolling underneath was both alien and eerily familiar, the airship's aging occupant mused. The occasional crater hove into view, plus mounds of sand shifting in the rarefied atmosphere. The sky was quite different, of course, from what this traveller remembered. One more journey across the cosmos, though a special one at that, the traveller thought to herself.

"We're getting close now," the traveller said to the fellow companion near the window. On hearing no response, the traveller thought the companion must be resting.

An adult Sophie was frantically pacing up and down a substantial atrium, gesticulating and muttering to an invisible opponent.

"Calm down, sis, or you will drill a hole through the floor," said her adult brother, Kevin.

"How can I calm down?" Sophie shot back. "Have you seen this message? Cameron, descendant of First Contact Commander Coleman Breen, has just cancelled. I mean this museum's inauguration is just hours away and her - the key member is not going to be there."

"You know you should eat something. When I have a problem, I like to work on a full stomach. Have you tried the new Galaxy Burgers…" Ethan started.

Sophie rounded on him angrily. "How can you think of food at a time like this!? We're on the verge of an interplanetary embarrassment and all you can think about is your stupid burger franchise!"

Seeing the genuine look of hurt across the face of normally jovial Ethan, Sophie immediately regretted her outburst.

"I'm sorry Tum, I know how hard you have worked to establish your burger chain, and how much of your profit margin has gone into this museum."

Ethan chuckled at his sister's nickname for him, and relaxed back to his jovial self. "Well, you know I need this museum to succeed as much as you – the food court will have a hard time selling in an empty building."

Their first museum visit for Sophie and Ethan, years ago now, where Sophie had first looked at the Bio Wars suit, had changed them both in different ways. Ethan had combined his love of food and passion for meeting people to develop a surprisingly successful food chain. He had followed his sister into the black on her exploratory trips, expanding his influence, and finances on the way. In the museum, following her meeting with chief historian, Sophie had decided on the spot that she wanted to become a research explorer. Her past journeys to the Martian Pyramids and the site of the Coleman Breen mission had led her to travel to the planet they were presently on.

"While you are enjoying the out-of-this-world taste of my latest Galaxy Burger, maybe you can remember when you fought to get a museum considered here in the first place."

Grabbing the proffered meal from her brother and eating like one half-starved, she remembered. Sophie, the historian graduate presenting to an audience vastly more experienced.

"The Scar is much like Mars, of the Pyramid fame," she began. "As some of you may know, the name comes from the thousands of kilometres long gash on the planet's crust where the air pressure is high enough to support an ecosystem with running water, vegetation and human habitation. The Scar was one of the first planets reached by an Exodus ship, though the society regressed quite quickly, probably within a generation." Sophie chose not to mention the politically sensitive Domer situation. The Domers were named after habitats established on the far less hospitable higher elevations, whose occupants had just lost a civil insurrection with the Scar People.

Sensing a subtle shift in her audience, Sophie hastily continued. "What you probably don't know – and that my team has just discovered - is that the Scar was within six months of being the site of First Contact between Earth and Irs."

Much of the audience sat up with interest.

Sophie stated: "From the Narriwa Legend, Irs sent hundreds of search-for-life interstellar probes in random directions as no one knew quite where to look. One of these made it to the Scar System, being almost halfway between Irs and Earth. It was no doubt attracted to transmissions from Scar's artificial Moon whose origin and purpose we still haven't figured out."

Sophie's presentation continued, demonstrating that a Terran deep space probe had also passed through the Scar system a mere six months earlier than the Irs ship.

"This planet was that close to changing history, though in a way it did," Sophie added.

"One of the Scar's first astronomers discovered the by-now defunct Irs probe in its strange orbit, starting a massive revolution in their understanding of science and the cosmos."

"And that Grand Pilot's telescope – you know, that 'famous' astronomer who you discovered, had murdered his father and took back the instrument from his dead hands - is now pride of place in your museum I believe," Ted broke through Sophie's remonstrance of the conference. "A fantastic way to progress science, killing the opposition, leading a revolution against the Grounders and forcing a new belief system on top."

"Maybe this whole museum is cursed, too close to Our Land," Sophie shrugged as she recited the language of the planet's ancestors while idly fingering the site of a repaired bullet hole. That had been another near-disaster following her near-kidnap by the Domers during the Museum planning phase. A combination of disinterested investors, civil unrest and unprofessional curators had almost killed someone. Sophie was overjoyed when news of a Bio War-era Boltzmann rifle, originating from the former Triton Refuelling Depot no less, was going to be in her museum. Distracted by yet another project delay, Sophie had let an inexperienced crew unpack and prepare the rifle for display. Somehow the ancient weapon had fired an equally ancient round, missing her head by millimetres.

The airship was nearing its final stop towards the edge of the Scar. A security detail deplaned and took up positions outside the ship to guard against any adverse activity. Just one more leg of the journey, the traveller thought, tiredly.

Bill followed Sophie on a last hurried inspection of the museum before the official opening. They passed under a huge flag from the Breen mission to Irs, and walked around a virtual viewing of the event that seemed to transport them to the monumental meeting.

As they passed another room containing an early surface lander, Ted leant to his sister's ear. "I see that the repairs to this area are finished as well."

Sophie blushed, remembering how awesome she had felt not only to secure a whole landing craft from the Herculis space ruins – the first ever evidence of extra-terrestrial activity ever found by Earth – but also to use a local Domer workforce to help with the installation. The Domers decided to show their gratitude by attempting to hijack the lander craft. Two Domers had climbed into the cockpit, and activated its ascent mode inside the museum. The centuries old vehicle instantly killed the remaining two Domers standing in the room with its rocket blast before hitting the roof, just as its obsolete launch system quit. Fortunately, the landing gear was designed to withstand twice the force of its crash landing, leaving a security team to extricate and unceremoniously throw out the shaken, but alive, Domers from the lander's cockpit. More repairs.

Unbelievably, these were not the worst of her misfortunes on this planet. Well before the museum was even planned, Sophie had held a second archaeological conference at the Scar. When enquiring about the Scar's preferred location for the conference for the second year in a row, senior organisers seemed rather vague in their answers. The best justification that Sophie could gather was that the Alliance would benefit from this planet being better known to scientists and scholars. It also transpired to be Sophie's last ever conference. She was partway through presenting on the final battle of Mortem

The artificial moon rises above the Scar, watched by two service craft. The moon's origin remains a mystery; historians believe it predates the Exodus.

in a question and answer session.

"…in fact Mortem's environment was so badly damaged that it was some time before the nascent space age of Irs could actually send a landing craft to its surface. The benefit of this, of course, was that it helped accelerate space industry advancement, eventually leading to development of the search-for-life probes that led to the discovery of our distant relatives. If you look at this time line…"

"Excuse me," came an interruption. "But weren't ruins of a space striker ship that participated in the war with Terra found on the surface of Mortem?"

"That's correct," Sophie replied. "The only damage we could see to its structure was due to exposure to Mortem's climate, so we think it was deliberately landed on the planet undamaged. We found…"

"And is it not a fact that the ruins are now residing in the Alliance museum on Terra and not anywhere near Irs? Do you think that is fair, Earth interfering yet again with our sacred heritage? The piece belongs to us!"

Murmurs of other audience members were getting louder as what seemed to be a professional agitator was raising the emotional level in the room.

Sophie tried her best to keep the conference at least resembling a professional gathering. "I am not sure about 'fair'; however I understand the artefact was donated to Earth as a sign of goodwill from the Irs government. I also know that Irs has similarly been given Terran-based artefacts."

The quick reflexes of her youth saved her life in the next instant. She threw herself backwards from her lectern as a weapon was suddenly brandished by one of her audience. The shot meant for her head instead impacted the display unit behind her, adding yet another crater to her displayed image of Mortem.

The next morning had seen Sophie travel directly to the space port, trying to secure the first flight out of there. Security forces had acted quickly to apprehend the would-be murderer, but for her, the turning of a supposedly esteemed conference into a farce was the last straw.

"I don't care about your technical problems, get me the first flight off this rock!" Sophie practically yelled at the booking coordinator.

"What's up sis?" came a familiar voice. "I can almost hear you on the other side of the planet."

"Tum! What are you doing here? Did you hear about the conference?" Sophie cheered somewhat at seeing her brother.

"Yes I heard, sorry about that. It is more or less why I'm here – that and Galaxy Burgers."

Sophie rolled her eyes and was about to turn back to organise her flight when he put a hand on her shoulder. "I have someone who would like to see you. It will only take a few minutes, and they have a chartered craft that can take you back home."

"Are you kidding me?!" Sophie shot back. "They will likely dump me out the airlock, if I don't get shot at again on the way to the transport! I am so over this dump!"

Ethan put on his most earnest gaze. "Trust me sis, you'll be ok. Don't look now but there are about ten security officers near you. Can you please do this one thing for me? It won't take long. Look, here is the representative now."

As Ethan spoke an unassuming man, foreign to the planet, Sophie thought, quietly came forward and beckoned Sophie to follow. She resigned herself to the inevitable and went with him, noticing part of the security detail following at a discrete distance.

The man quietly led Sophie through a series of ever more confusing small corridors, rooms and turns until she became thoroughly lost. Seeing that Ethan had somehow made himself scarce, she was about the collar her mysterious companion when she almost collided with the Irs First Minister.

"Sorry for the subterfuge but please take a seat." He said as Sophie looked about to faint.

Half collapsing into one of four chairs, the most senior government representatives of Earth and Mars suddenly appeared sitting in the other seats. Part of Sophie knew that what she was seeing were virtual representations of the ministers who were most likely physically located on their home worlds, but to her senses, they appeared real.

The Terran First minister spoke. "Sophie, I appreciate that you are very keen to return home, but we are wondering if we could take a little of your time to ask for your help."

"Y-Yes of course minister," Sophie gulped, wondering what Ethan had to do with any of this.

The Mars representative then spoke. "You have experienced first-hand how fragile our Galactic Alliance actually is, given the sensitivities surrounding the discoveries of the interstellar war."

The Irs First Minister spoke next. "The Scar, representing a mid-point between Terra and Irs, is struggling to fully integrate with the Alliance. It possesses ideal conditions for the growth of violent separatists, and we don't mean the Domers."

"Not the Domers?" Sophie blurted out.

The Mars First Minister spoke next. "No, the Domer unrest has simply provided a reasonable hiding place for these separatists to operate. The one who tried to shoot you yesterday was not a Domer, but a hard-core separatist. The unfolding issue here is affecting the whole Alliance, which is why we are here to ask for your help to build a new museum of history on the Scar."

Building a museum, surprising as the notion was, made sense to Sophie. The relocation of artefacts collected throughout the Alliance at this half-way location would negate arguments over historic favouritism. It would also provide an attractive tourist destination for this region, and if local workforce was used in its construction, more political stability.

"But why me?" Sophie stammered. "I'm just a line-research manager. Surely Laura of Pyramid fame, or Freya or Phrane are more qualified, and more well-known."

The Terran Minister answered. "Laura specifically recommended you for your emerging reputation, as did Freya and Phrane. We all believed their public status may lead to partisan dissent, whereas a relative newcomer, the attempt on your life notwithstanding, might be seen as more neutral. They will provide whatever assistance you may need of course."

The Mars First Minister continued. "With regards to your safety, Domer representatives have come forward to condemn the violence at the conference and are actively working with our security teams to apprehend separatists. It seems that there are elements in their ranks who would like to see the end of violence as much as we would."

Two years later, the Galactic Alliance got their wish. Sophie led the museum construction effort. Apart from Boltzmann accident and the attempted hijacking from what turned out to be a separatist-organised operation, the project had run smoothly. Until now.

Sophie and Ethan were just passing into another area containing the recovered almost-first-contact Irs alien probe when Sophie got an urgent call. "The Minister for the museum opening is here," she said to her brother. "And I still don't have a keynote speaker!"

"I'm sure everything will go ok, but best not to keep the Minister waiting," replied Ethan a little too calmly. Sophie was about to shoot back at him but he was already hurrying to the front of the museum.

This is it, she thought gloomily. Years of planning and building a project intended to unite the Domers and Scar People into the Alliance was about to become the biggest embarrassment this world had seen. As Sophie rounded the bend to the main entrance she almost ran into two Domer workers

Generations of fighters roaring out of yesteryear greet visitors to Sophie's museum. They are flanked by a Bio Wars soldier, representing a period of conflict, and a spacesuited figure representing a new era of peaceful exploration.

struggling with a large crate.

"A new museum acquisition coming in just before the official opening?" she started thinking before she heard her name called. Sophie's parents had just appeared from behind the work crew and crate.

"Sorry we're a little late; we got caught up in Customs coming through. Something to do with the Minister I expect."

"It's so good to see you," said Sophie, but there is a little hitch. I've lost the key member. How do I open without her? What will I tell the Minister?"

Ethan coughed. "Oh, sorry, forgot to mention, sis. I've taken care of that, care of the new Galaxy Burger flavour that really brings people together."

Sophie looked like she would have shot her brother if she still possessed the ancient Boltzmann, but she rapidly composed herself as the Minister strode forward, accompanied by an unassuming lady. The aging traveller had finally arrived, and was clearly enjoying the Scar's reduced gravity.

The Minister, descendent of the line of Grand Pilots and mediator of the aftermath of Scar's civil war stepped forward to introduce his companion.

"Sophie, please allow me to introduce you to our key member and somebody you may already be familiar with."

The young woman gasped and stammered. "Jordan? The sole Pyramid survivor from Mars? Welcome…but how...?"

Jordan smiled and winked. "All in good time – I'll tell you all about it later. We had better get on with opening this museum of yours."

The next events were a blur to Sophie. The Minister gave his introductory speech, and then it was her turn. She could hardly remember what she said, though Ethan assured her after the event that it seemed quite good.

Jordan, her new keynote speaker, then moved to address the gathered audience. "Thank you for inviting me to your planet to open the new Museum of History," she began. "The planet I come from, Mars, is about the same size as the Scar. Like many here who experienced the recent civil war and other unrest, we Martians watched as the clouds of war quickly gathered around us. Soon all of our small population was helping our equally small military prepare for the inevitable. I was a junior battle analyst working to support our force leader, Shadom, prepare to defend Mars against the impending attack. Not many of us really understood what cause could possibly justify why so-called advanced civilizations wanted to risk humanity's total annihilation.

As many of the artefacts and records in this museum show, we on Mars fought very bravely and were defeated very quickly. My small world's ecosystem vanished and, through reasons I can't explain, I am now the only survivor of that horrible, interstellar war.

I no longer recognize the faces of Earth or even my own planet Mars. The weapons used in that war erased my history. Everyone and everything I ever knew has vanished, or is forever entombed in the Martian pyramids. I have come to personally know the cost of thinking only of one's own interests. I can tell you from my experience that if humanity fails to work together, if the Galactic Alliance that has cost us all dearly, fails to work, then there will be no winners in the next conflict, just like there were no victors in the last."

Jordan gestured for the crate she had brought with her to the stage. Very carefully, the contents were extracted for the audience to see. Inside was a rectangular casket, the semi-transparent covering of which revealed what looked like a young girl fast asleep. For a long moment there was silence, until Jordan finally spoke.

"Her modern name was Clarissa, the girl I saw killed in the last stages of the attacks on Mars. Before she died Clarissa told me that she had wanted to travel, to see the universe. We hope that bringing Clarissa to rest here, close to where the war began, will help us all remember that while humanity is physically separated, we are still one people."

Collective, introspective silence gave way to loud applause as Jordan's words hit home. Signals sent simultaneously from the Alliance home worlds commanded a lock on the front doors to de-activate, officially marking the museum's public opening.

Many hours after the opening ceremony, deemed a huge success by all present, Jordan was alone with the casket containing Clarissa. The museum was empty; even Sophia had left to join another ceremony celebrating the joint museum venture. Below a series of sculptures chronicling the history of the Pyramids and their relation to the Scar, Jordan said her last goodbyes to Clarissa. She knew that the girl, whose life was robbed thousands of years ago, was finally at rest. Neither machinery nor evil could hurt her anymore.

(Above) The formal ceremony over, Sophie views the newly-opened museum on the Scar. It was became a popular destination for locals and interstellar visitors. The museum also firmly concluded the vestiges of the civil unrest between seperatist factions on the planet.

www.ingramcontent.com/pod-product-compliance
Lightning Source LLC
Chambersburg PA
CBHW041158300726
48981CB00004B/295